KV-730-438

LAWMEN

Tom Ford, the sheriff of Stanton, was gunned down while trying to keep the peace between the hands of rival ranches. News of Tom Ford's death reaches his son, Chris, and Marshal Sam Ward while they are hunting down a killer. Chris returns home to face his past and to find his father's killer and for this he must take up his father's badge — only to discover that not everything is as it seems . . .

JACK GILES

LAWMEN

Complete and Unabridged

LINFORD
Leicester

First published in Great Britain in 2008 by
Robert Hale Limited
London

First Linford Edition
published 2009
by arrangement with
Robert Hale Limited
London

The moral right of the author
has been asserted

Copyright © 2008 by Jack Giles
All rights reserved

British Library CIP Data

Giles, Jack.
    Lawmen- -(Linford western library)
    1. Western stories.
    2. Large type books.
    I. Title II. Series
    823.9′14–dc22

    ISBN 978–1–84782–773–9

ROTHERHAM LIBRARY &
INFORMATION SERVICES

B52036099S

TTL579906

Published by
F. A. Thorpe (Publishing)
Anstey, Leicestershire

Set by Words & Graphics Ltd.
Anstey, Leicestershire
Printed and bound in Great Britain by
T. J. International Ltd., Padstow, Cornwall

This book is printed on acid-free paper

1

'Hell's teeth!' Sam Ward exploded. 'You can't just go swannin' off. We got us a job to do.'

'The hell I can't,' his companion retorted. 'Figure I can just do what I damn well want. This is family business — an' where I come from that's what comes first.'

'But we've got to bring in Fogarty first, Chris,' Sam responded, his originally firm order now edging towards a whining plea.

'Liam Fogarty?' the younger man, Chris Ford, spat. 'He'll be long gone. I figure we're just on a flamin' wild-goose chase. Every time we close in we've been given the go-around and told he's gone this way an' that. All he is is a two-bit rustler.'

'A two-bit rustler who killed a man,' Sam reminded him sternly, surprised that this fact had escaped his deputy's memory.

Chris stared thoughtfully off into the middle distance as though the answer to his dilemma lay there. Maybe he could have worded the announcement that he was about to break up their partnership a bit better. Though, he admitted to himself, he should have been aware that his decision invited the reaction that he had got.

'Make you a deal,' he offered at length. 'If he's not in the next town we go our separate ways.'

Sam gave his companion a thoughtful glance. Even he believed, like Chris, that they were on nothing more than a wild-goose chase. They had got close, but a series of mishaps, which had been his own fault, had caused them to lose their quarry. Now they were traipsing across a barren landscape in the faint hope that they would, eventually, track Fogarty down.

'Anyhows, you ain't said what's so damn important that you got to head off?' He decided to change the subject.

'Family problems,' Chris answered, his tone indicating that it was none of the older man's business.

Family problems; he grimaced as he thought of the message that had at last caught up with him in the previous town. His father had been gunned down in an altercation with some rowdy cowhands. It was as simple as that. What concerned him more was that his mother was all alone now and would be waiting for her boys to come home. No doubt his elder brother, Charlie, would be getting compassionate leave from the Army and Hal, the youngest of them, well, he'd just down tools and was in all probability already home, or in spitting distance.

'Hell, Chris,' Sam said, interrupting his thoughts. 'Give me some idea — you ain't sayin' nothin'.'

'Ain't your business,' Chris told him. Then, reluctantly, he reached into his back pocket and produced a crumpled piece of paper.

For a moment he stood there, undecided, his eyes scanning the brief telegram. It was reasonable, he concluded, that his boss was owed an explanation for his departure, for Chris was never one to leave with bad feelings hanging behind him. So he handed the scrap of paper down to Sam, who shifted uncomfortably on the tree stump that formed his seat.

Sam took it and opened the sheet and, squinting at the words, read the message. The simple statement made him grimace before he handed it back.

'Well, I figure that there ain't a choice in the matter,' Sam conceded, standing up and rubbing his numb backside. 'You gotta do what's gotta be done.'

'Was goin' to anyways,' Chris stated. 'Even if it meant me handin' in my badge.'

'Couldn't let you do that,' Sam stated, gruffly. 'You're too damn good a man to lose.'

Chris could only nod, an admission that the older man was right for they had worked as a team for the past five years as marshal and deputy. Two men who knew their territory and rarely lost their quarry.

Liam Fogarty seemed to be one man who was going to go into the loss column of their book — but he would only be the third name in that list. They had covered all his usual haunts and found him to be one step ahead of them. Now they were heading further than Fogarty had been known to go and in a northerly direction. It would have been more likely that he would have gone south with the Mexican border in mind and well out of the marshal's jurisdiction. But instead he was heading for the railway at Dennett Junction. That destination, in its own way, raised the question — why?

There was nothing there. Just an old livery where the stage stop had been and a hotel-cum-saloon that had seen better days, some cattle pens and a tall wooden warehouse where freight wagons would gather when the trains came in. The junction was nothing more than a stopover point where travellers waited to change trains or freighters picked up their cargo.

There could be the only one reason that Fogarty would head there, and that was to catch a train. Both men knew it and had no reason to voice it.

Instead, Sam Ward climbed off the stump and rubbed his numb backside into life. Stomping around to loosen up his legs he used the energy to swipe dirt into the embers of their campfire. While he was doing that Chris slipped off his red plaid three-quarter-length jacket, which he folded neatly and placed on top of his bedroll. Then hefted up his saddle and blanket and prepared to saddle his horse. Methodically and meticulously he checked the girths and the bridle, making sure that neither would make the horse uncomfortable.

It always came as a surprise to Sam, the way that his deputy always paid so much attention to detail. Therefore he was somewhat surprised that Chris had forgotten that Fogarty was a killer. Though, now that he knew that Chris had other things on his mind, he could find that lapse understandable. He, also, had to concede that they might have not lasted so long together if Chris had not taken time to think things through.

Chris buttoned up his brown leather vest, with its shiny silver deputy's badge pinned over his heart, and made sure that it was snug against his light-blue denim shirt before strapping on a scuffed gunbelt. Out of habit he whipped out his pistol, checked that it was in full working condition and loaded before sliding it back into the holster.

After adjusting the flat brim of his low-crowned black hat over a shock of straw-coloured hair he turned to complete the chores of tying his bedroll and jacket to the back of the saddle and slipping his rifle into the boot.

He was all set and ready to continue the hopeless pursuit, unlike Sam, who always seemed to labour away at the easiest of chores. They were plainly two men who were like chalk and cheese. While Chris was neat and well-presented Sam sported a battered high-crowned hat, from beneath which sprouted long, greying hair, a dustcoat that had seen better days, a grey shirt and black baggy trousers tucked into brown cowboy boots. Still, there were twenty-three years between their ages and Chris had to concede that the older man had been about and was, there-fore, far more experienced in the ways of life. Nor did it matter to Chris what a man looked like; it was what he did that was the main concern — and Sam was no slouch when it came to watching Chris's back.

'Well, if nuthin' else,' Sam remarked, climbing into the saddle, 'we get to Dennet Junction then I'll get me a bath and a shave.'

'Thought you were goin' to grow a beard?' Chris mentioned as he steered his horse on to the main track.

Sam rubbed his bristles and grimaced: 'Thought about it. Right now it feels damn uncomfortable and it itches like hell.'

'Got no sympathy.' Chris grinned easily, rubbing his own chin.

'Well, you ain't got nothin' to brag about,' Sam pointed out. 'You got three days of fuzz there that needs hacking off.'

'At least I'll use a razor,' Chris responded. 'Not wire cutters.'

Sam nodded. He was just glad that they were back to their old bantering way and that the past uneasiness was behind him. Yet he was fully aware that he was going to miss the youngster when they parted company at the Junction. They both knew that the trail would go cold at that point and, whichever way he went, Fogarty would be heading across the line.

'Were you close?' Sam asked into the silence that had developed between them.

'What?' Chris asked, taken unawares

and unsure to what his partner was referring.

'You and your pa,' Sam expanded. 'Were you close?'

Close? Chris almost sneered aloud.

Close as the middle child runt could get, he supposed. In looks and build he had followed his mother. His two brothers had been well-built and almost six foot by the time they were fourteen — while he had been just five and a half feet tall at that age. Since then he had added another three inches. His brothers were workers while he liked to read. His father had despised his intelligence and was jealous of the way he could solve problems.

His father had been a carpenter but, no matter how hard he tried, Chris could never saw through a piece of wood following a straight line, unlike Charlie and Hal, who took to working with their hands as though it was the natural thing to do.

When Chris first decided to leave home and find his own way his father had been scathing. He couldn't see his son surviving in the outside world. When Chris did make the break he just proved his father wrong.

'Sorry,' Sam muttered, breaking into Chris's thoughts. 'Just interested.'

'Grateful for the concern,' Chris answered, his tone impassive. 'Whatever I may feel, he was my father and it doesn't matter whether we were close or not, he's still dead.'

'Not looking for revenge, are you?' Sam asked, cautiously.

Chris shook his head: 'Got two brothers who will be and that'll worry Ma.'

For a moment he hesitated wondering why he was talking so openly when all he wanted was to be left alone with his thoughts. Revenge was not something that was on his mind, but he did want his father's killer brought to justice.

'Not too bothered, for now,' Chris continued, not wanting to declare his thoughts. 'Ma would've mentioned something if she knew who did the killin'.'

'Maybe.' Sam shrugged, deciding not to go into a philosophical debate on the subject. He saw no point in going into an 'ifs and buts' conversation; this was something for his young deputy to sort out in his mind. Besides, another thought had occurred to him, that linked to an earlier conversation.

'You know, I was thinking,' Sam commented.

'Dangerous that,' Chris responded quickly. 'Thinking can seriously damage the brain.'

'Figured that.' Sam chuckled before returning to his thoughts. 'You remember we chased Matt Jaeger until he disappeared into the mountains?'

Chris nodded as he recalled the incident. They had been chasing the leader of a gang of rustlers, who had plagued the area for several years, and who had managed to give them the slip. One minute Jaeger had had them pinned down and the next he had just upped and disappeared. Although they had searched the known tracks, when they had come down to the edge of the desert the chase came to a dead end.

'Strange that,' Chris said, wondering where this line of thought was going.

'It's just that Fogarty rode with Jaeger,' Sam mentioned, a comment that made his companion frown.

'Just a coincidence,' Chris decided without much conviction.

'Don't know why I never thought of this before,' Sam continued, as though Chris hadn't spoken. 'But you ever wondered where the cattle that Fogarty stole went?'

'South?' Chris questioned, just as another idea came to mind. 'Or is that what we were supposed to think?'

'Now that you mention it,' Sam acknowledged, 'Fogarty's movements certainly suggest he'd been down Mexico way.'

'There's more to this than meets the eye,' Chris mused. 'If I remember right

Cap Turner got gunned down in Mexico by some bounty hunter. He was riding with Jaeger at one time.'

'I saw the body,' Sam reminded his deputy. 'So Turner's out of it. But I guess you've got something goin' with the way you're thinkin'. I mean Jaeger must be around someplace an' Fogarty's makin' things hot for himself — guess the two of them are going to lock up someplace.'

Chris nodded: 'That's what I was comin' to. If they're at Dennett Junction we get the chance to square the books.'

'That's one hell of a big if,' Sam mused. 'But, like you, I think Fogarty'll be long gone. East, west or north on a train to someplace.'

'Won't be east,' Chris opined grimly, with a shake of his head. 'Nothin' there for him. His business is cattle — so I figure he'd go west or north and look for a place where he's not on a Wanted dodger.'

Both men rode on in silence for a

while, each engrossed in his own thoughts.

Sam had no intention of letting Fogarty get away with murder. If necessary he would try to enlist the aid of the local law in his hunt. He just regretted that he would not have Chris to back him up. Still, the kid had his own problems and Sam could not help but understand that they came first.

Chris's mind was not on his own problems. It was the business in hand that bothered him, and the fact that Sam would be returning empty handed while he, Chris, went home to care for his mother. Maybe, he reasoned, they might get lucky and find Fogarty at Dennett Junction. Though the thought might have seemed far-fetched, he was well aware that stranger things had happened. Like the time when they had discovered that a bank robber was staying at a hotel right under their noses. It had been the quickest arrest that they had ever made; no one had expected the man to remain at the scene of his crime.

He narrowed his eyes, following the way that the trail curved across the barren landscape. In the distance he could see a grey smudge on the horizon, which indicated that Dennett Junction was just a handful of miles away.

No one could quite understand how the Junction had got its name. To most people the place should have been named Gingell Junction, for Pete Gingell had run the way station long before the railroad had come there. Still did, as the stage would pull in at the station to collect those passengers who were heading south.

But some man named Abe Dennett had, supposedly, struck the last spike on completion of the junction and it had borne his name ever since.

'I see it,' Sam grumbled, wiping a gloved hand across his whiskers.

He had anticipated the youngster before the pointing finger was half-raised.

'Can't wait, huh?' Chris remarked with a grin as he dropped his hand.

'Civilization?' Sam growled. 'Not what it's cracked up to be. Wonder if I can get a shave without someone wantin' to know my life story?' He glanced at the sky. 'Just once, Lord, just once.'

'Never took you for a religious man,' Chris observed, giving his companion a quizzical glance.

'I'm not,' Sam fired back. 'Just once in a while I get to hopin' that one of them up there is listenin' in and taking notice. That's the biggest drawback with this job. It don't matter who you meet — barber, barkeep or shopkeeper — they either want to bore you with all their little woes or want to know your business.'

'That's life, Sam,' Chris replied. 'Live with it. It's what gets me through.'

'That's what I reckoned.' Sam chuckled. 'When I was your age.'

The first thing that they noticed was that there had been changes at Dennett

Junction since they had last ridden by. A single-storey general store now stood alongside the two-storey hotel-cum-saloon, behind which was a new bathhouse.

'Someone's been busy,' Sam remarked as they dismounted and hitched their horses to the post outside the saloon.

'That's not all,' Chris stated, pointing over to the plot of land alongside the warehouse. 'Got something pegged out over there.'

'Some fellers goin' to build a factory there,' a voice behind them remarked, making them turn around to face the speaker.

He was a short, rotund man wearing a dark-grey three-piece suit and a black hat with a curled brim.

'Name's Ralph Maguire,' he introduced himself, nervously using a big white handkerchief to wipe sweat from his face. 'I'm a surveyor. And you are looking at the future of Dennett Junction.'

'It has a future?' Sam responded with incredulity.

'Yes, sir,' Maguire replied, waving the handkerchief expansively around him. 'What we have here is a junction and there are big interests back East, who want to invest in factories out here. They want homes for their workers and they want stores. I can tell you that in less than a year you won't recognize the place.'

'Shame, that.' Sam shrugged, disappointment evident in his tone.

'Why's that?' asked Maguire with a perplexed expression.

'We don't like change,' Chris replied by way of explanation. 'Somehow it messes things up.'

His eyes were steady on the man's face; he appeared to be sweating a lot. Beads ran down his face to drip from the end of his nose and chin. Also, Maguire's appearance and speech struck Chris as a little too speedy and false.

'There has to be . . . ' Maguire stumbled and faltered, aware that neither man was paying much attention to him.

'Tell me later,' Sam snapped decisively, unimpressed by the other man's enthusiasm for change. 'I've got other things to attend to.'

Without waiting for a response Sam strode towards the station. There he found the stationmaster busy sweeping dust from the boarded platform. He glanced up on hearing boot-heels thumping the boards as Sam strode determinedly towards the stooped, grey-haired man.

Pete Gingell was a proud man and valued his position as stationmaster, as he had once been while running the way station. Progress had helped to age him but had done nothing to hinder his own ambitions. While he ran the station it was his son and Pete's wife who ran the hotel; and his first grandson and *his* wife who had built and owned the general store. After training to become a competent blacksmith the second grandson had taken charge of the livery stable. It had to be said that Pete Gingell was proud of his little family business.

'See that feller collared you.' Gingell spat on the ground for emphasis.

'Yeah, seems your little empire's about to be invaded,' Sam commented ruefully.

'Progress,' Gingell hissed the word out. 'That's what that Maguire feller says. Reckons I'm gonna benefit from it. That's what they said when they built this here railroad. I ain't no better off now than when I was changing horses for the stage.' He paused to give a long look at both Sam and Chris before asking the inevitable question. 'So what brings you to Progress, Sam? You gonna be the law up here?'

'No, Pete, we were following Liam Fogarty,' Sam became official, though he smiled wryly at the station man's sarcastic renaming of the town. 'Looked like he was heading this way. Tall feller around six two with rusty hair and a face that looks all beaten up.'

'Stands out, don't he,' Pete Gingell remarked. 'I know Fogarty from the old days. Yeah, he was up here. Met up with a couple of fellers and bought a ticket up to Lattimer. 'Cept I don't think he was headin' that far.'

'What makes you think that?' Sam asked, conversationally.

'Took his horse with him,' Gingell replied. 'It's a hundred mile or more to Lattimer and he weren't carryin' no feed for the horse.'

'And the next stop is?' Sam prompted.

'Carfax,' Chris supplied. 'And that's cattle country up there.'

'Figures.' Sam nodded, his memory being jogged at the mention of cattle. 'When's the next train in that direction?'

'Three days' time,' Gingell's reply was immediate. 'Pulls in here at ten in the mornin'.'

'It'll take us less than that to ride up that way,' Chris remarked, his mind more on keeping on the move. Thoughts that troubled him were beginning to form.

Sam turned to face his deputy: 'Thought you had something else to do? Besides, Carfax is outside our jurisdiction.'

'Carfax won't be going out of my way,' Chris stated curtly, for a certain gut feeling, which he was not yet ready to share, was beginning to grow.

Without another word he turned away and strode back towards the saloon. A perplexed Sam exchanged questioning glances with Pete Gingell.

'Don't ask,' Sam warned the station-master.

'Wasn't goin' to.' Gingell shrugged and turned back to his chore.

Chris wasted no time. He plunged through the batwing doors with a force that left them flapping in his wake. His eyes raked the dark interior, but the only people he saw were the barkeep behind the counter and the surveyor slumped down as though trying to make himself invisible in a shadowy corner.

'Wasn't his fault,' the barkeep offered,

his voice low but loud enough to make Chris turn and face him.

He was of average appearance and very nondescript-looking, the kind of person who would not stand out in a crowd. Even here in the saloon he was just anonymous — just a familiar face that could be instantly forgotten.

'What wasn't?' the deputy asked, slowly approaching the bar.

'There was a feller with a gun on him,' the barkeep continued. 'And another by the window, taking a long gander at the two of you. Feller seemed to know who you were.'

Chris nodded. It explained why the fat surveyor had been sweating so much and had gabbled his spiel about the town expanding.

'And you?' Chris demanded. 'Where were you?'

'Right here.' The barkeep shrugged. 'Got no other place to be. 'Sides, the feller at the window had his gun aimed at me. I wasn't goin' to risk getting' killed.'

'Yeah, right,' Chris responded, sarcastically. 'So where are they now?'

The barkeep just shrugged: 'How'd the hell I know? They just lit out and ain't come back.'

'They — they said something about going to — to the livery,' the surveyor offered, stumbling over his words.

As he spoke Sam came through the doors and, like Chris before him, took in his surroundings before bellying up to the bar.

'Two beers,' was all he said before turning to Chris. 'You going to join me? Or you just going to stand there keeping the cards close to your chest?'

'There's a couple of hopefuls checking us out,' Chris told him. 'I think we need to deal with that problem before we do anything else.'

Sam sighed: 'Got a location?'

'Livery — maybe.'

Sam shook his head: 'If that's where they are they could've taken us both out when we came back from the station.'

'Maybe.' Chris nodded. 'But I think

they want to be sure they get the both of us together.'

Sam pushed his duster away from his hip, exposing his holstered pistol. While he was doing that Chris slid his own gun out, checked it and held it against his side. He was no quick-draw artist and preferred his gun to be in his hand for instant use should it prove necessary.

'Ready?' Sam asked, with a slight cock of his eyebrows.

'As I'll ever be,' Chris confirmed, taking a step towards the door.

Sam went through first and didn't stop until he reached the dirt road outside the saloon. Covering him, Chris swung around and stood firm on the boardwalk. Together they probed the street with their eyes, searching for the slightest movement or shadow where there shouldn't be one. It was deathly quiet out on the street, where nothing stirred, but both men knew that the silence was deceptive. A sudden movement by the station caught their eyes. Pete Gingell stood in the open office doorway both arms stretched out with fingers pointing at the livery and the warehouse. Then he disappeared, but not before Sam had acknowledged the signal by saluting, with a finger tapping the brim of his hat.

Chris stepped down from the boardwalk. Moving behind Sam he angled his way across the street so that he could get a view of both the livery stable and the warehouse. Both men stood there holding their ground and waiting. If anyone was going to make a move it was going to be down to the opposition.

They didn't have to wait long before the two gunmen came running from their hiding places with guns drawn and blazing.

Sam shook his head as he watched dirt spurt up in the road where the bullets fell short of their target. Shots fired from unsteady hands as the two gunmen bore down on the stationary targets. Concentrating on the man sprinting up from the livery, Sam waited until his target was in range before exploding two shots that forced him to his knees. The body rocked once before falling forward into the dust.

Seeing his partner go down, the other man skidded to a halt to stare at the body. Then he attempted to backtrack, firing his gun in an attempt to take Sam down as he did so. Chris fired three shots and the second man staggered back like an off-balance drunkard who had tripped over his feet, before falling to lie spread-eagled on his back.

Covering the two bodies, Sam and Chris checked them out before holstering their guns. Unceremoniously, Sam put his boot into the crumpled body of the man whom he had killed, so that it rolled over on its back.

'That's Val Decker,' Sam noted, pointing at the spread-eagled body. 'The other's Hank Sweet. Both worked with Fogarty.'

'Guess Fogarty doesn't want us to follow him,' Chris observed. He slipped out his gun and opened the gate to replace the used bullets.

'Figured that,' Sam commented. He turned around and headed for the saloon. 'I could do with that beer now.'

He moved fast, without waiting for Chris, for he did not want the deputy to see that his hands were shaking. Only he was aware that for a moment he had frozen and come close to death. Only instinct had kept him alive.

2

'Still can't get over it,' Sam commented over breakfast.

They were all seated around a huge oak dining table at the back of the saloon: Pete Gingell, his wife, his son and two grandsons, the barkeeper and the surveyor, along with Sam and Chris.

'What's that?' Chris asked, knowing what would come next for the topic had become repetitious.

He had gone through the whole thing while they had bathed, shaved and eaten a filling meal the night before. Chris had just been grateful that they had had separate rooms, for he was certain that otherwise he would have got no sleep.

'Those guys running straight at us like that,' Sam said with a shake of his head.

'Figure they just wanted to surprise you,' Pete Gingell suggested, trying to keep his tone light, for he had overheard the whole story during dinner.

'Con-confuse you, perhaps,' the still nervous surveyor put in. 'That . . . that could've been their intention.'

'What's it matter, Sam?' Chris asked in a firm attempt to close the subject. 'They're dead and we're alive — and that's all that matters.'

'Boy's right,' Pete Gingell pointed out. 'Never seen no point in dwellin' on all the what 'n' whys. Life goes on and while you're thinking about it something else passes by.'

'Never known you to be so philosophical,' Sam responded, surprised at the station man's comment.

'Come to that,' Pete countered, looking meaningfully at him, 'never known you to worry a thing to death, either.'

'Getting old, I guess,' Chris said thoughtfully, unaware that he had voiced his own concerns.

'Fifty ain't old,' Sam spat back indignantly, his eyebrows lowering into a hurt scowl.

'You're as old as you feel,' the surveyor chimed in, gaining a little confidence from the easy-going banter.

'I feel a lot of things, feller,' Sam barked at him. 'Old ain't one of them.'

'Good for you, Sam.' Chris grinned, starting to rise from the table. 'As you're feeling a mite sprightly maybe we should be making a move. Unless, of course, you'd rather wait for the train.'

'I thought we were going our separate ways,' Sam reminded his deputy.

'Carfax won't be taking me out of my way,' Chris assured him.

Sam nodded, not totally convinced of Chris's honesty. Ever since Carfax had been mentioned the young deputy had acted as though he knew something that he wasn't sharing. This attitude was nothing new, however, for Chris had held back on a hunch before, until he was certain that he had the facts to back it up.

It was for this reason that Chris was, indeed, holding back. He was aware of the implications if Carfax was Fogarty's destination, for that town was situated some thirty miles away from his own home town of Stanton.

Carfax was known for its cattle depots and lay on the edges of some prime grazing owned by several big ranch owners. The coming of the railroad had turned the small cowtown into a boom town boasting a grid of streets that almost made it comparable to a small city.

It was clear in his mind that Fogarty was either shifting his base of operations and was about to start targeting fresh fields, or was just planning on losing himself in the bustling side streets. Chris had enough to bother about when he returned home without having to worry about trouble getting there ahead of him.

'What's going through that head of yours?' Sam asked, once they had left the saloon and were walking up the boardwalk towards the livery.

'Just trying to figure out what Fogarty's up to.' Chris shrugged as he skirted a trio of rockers that barred the way.

'I can tell you that,' Sam grumbled. 'He don't want us following him. Why else would he have a couple of gunhands waiting for us? Damn fools — still can't figure why — '

'They acted like they did,' Chris finished for him as he turned to his partner. 'You've done all that to death. Forget about it — or go find some medicine man who talks to the dead. Then you can ask them why they did it.'

'Hell's teeth, Chris,' Sam barked in a hurt tone. 'Quit yelling at me.'

'I'm not . . . ' Chris felt exasperated but lowered his tone, 'yelling. It's just that you've got this one topic of conversation that's getting just a little bit boring.'

'But . . . ' Sam protested, flapping his

arms outwards in some vague gesture.

He could not explain the way he felt. It was as though something heavy had suddenly closed on him and was beginning to crush him. Suddenly he lurched to one side and had to stretch out a hand to lean against the wooden saloon wall just to keep him upright.

This moment was missed by Chris who, having had enough, spun on his heel with the intention of walking off. The intention was short-lived as, with second thoughts, he turned back to Sam.

'They're dead and we're alive,' Chris pointed out, stabbing a finger at Sam's chest. 'That's all I need to know. If you need to chew on something, then try and figure out Fogarty's next move.'

'It ain't that,' Sam confessed, slumping into one of the rockers at the end of the boardwalk. 'I just stood there like a damn fool with bullets flying around me. Decker took me off guard. By rights I should be dead. I just stood there watching him run at me and, suddenly, I realized that if I didn't do something fast I'd be dead. Maybe I *am* getting too old for this job.'

'Fifty ain't old,' Chris echoed Sam's own words, trying to reassure him.

'And that's a lie,' Sam admitted. 'Come next January I'll be sixty and that's the truth. Sooner or later someone'll figure it out and I'll be pensioned off. I don't want that, Chris. Those damn fools — hell's teeth, I could've got you killed.'

Chris squatted down to sit on his heels and looked at the grey-faced man sitting in the rocker.

'Like I said, Sam, we're both alive,' he said, softly. 'You took Decker down — not me, and he was kissing the dirt before Sweet. I didn't see you do anything wrong.'

He stood up and glanced down towards the livery, mentally debating what to do next. It would have been easy to walk off and go to Carfax alone. If it was necessary he would still do that — but five years with Sam had taught him that walking away would not be the done thing.

'Right, Sam, you've had your say,' Chris's tone was sharp. He stood up and bent over the older man, his hands gripping the arms of the rocker. 'Now you and me have got a job to do and we'll take it as far as we can get it. It's what we do — what we've always done. That's who we are. Why we work well together. So you lied about your age — does that change who you are?'

Sam sprang up from the chair with a force that almost sent Chris sprawling.

'Who the hell do you think you are?' Sam roared. 'Who gave you the right to lecture me?'

'You did.' Chris grinned, relieved that the old man was getting fired up again. 'The moment you started wallowing.'

'But it's the truth,' Sam protested vigorously. 'I'm slowing up. There was a time when it would have been me that would have figured out something was wrong. But you had it worked out and you did something about it. You knew that someone was laying for us.'

'Suspected,' Chris corrected him. 'A fat man sweating? In this heat I'd expect the same. No, it was his spiel — too quick and nervous. He's a surveyor, remember, not a salesman.'

'Yeah, I noticed that, too,' Sam admitted. 'But I was all fired up and all I wanted to know was where Fogarty had gone.'

'I wanted to know that as well,' Chris stated. 'So what? All it tells me is that we both ignored the danger signals and went off to do what we had to do. Let's face it, if we hadn't then that surveyor and the barkeep might've been killed in a shoot-out.' In an unusual show of affection he grabbed hold of Sam's arm. 'We've ridden together for five years — I sure as hell know you ain't no more fifty now than you were back then. So if it don't matter to me it shouldn't matter to you.'

'That's the trouble,' Sam confessed, releasing himself from Sam's grasp. 'It does matter to me. I'm slowing down

— not reacting fast enough. And I'm standing next to some damn kid who can do the job a darn sight better than me.' Then, realizing that he had paid a compliment, he cuffed Chris on the shoulder. 'Like hell you can. Guess we'd better finish this job — together.'

'About time you got around to thinking right.' Chris grinned. 'We spend much more time hanging around here jawing that next train'll be in Carfax before we've made a move.'

Sam knew that Chris was right. They had a job to do and he was determined to see it through. Though this wasn't enough to silence that niggling thought in the back of his mind that he had frozen at a vital moment. It was, he decided, easier to accept the excuse that it was the sudden surprise of the attack that had taken him off guard.

Also, his self-esteem had been boosted when Chris had suggested that they finish the job together. For he feared the youngster's departure, which would leave him alone. He had, in the last few minutes, come to realize just how much he depended on Chris. To discover, after all these years, that there were others who depended on the deputy had also caused him to feel that little bit jealous.

Chris had never talked about his family, from which Sam had deduced that the boy he had taken under his wing was just another orphan. But then, at first Sam had been a little slow in coming forward about himself and had busied himself with honing the boy's skills. Despite the age difference they had bonded well and had become a formidable team.

That thought put confidence into his stride as he caught up with his partner and together they entered the livery.

'Hey, Sam,' Chris said, as they finished saddling their mounts, 'you go on ahead. Looks like I forgot my coat.'

'It's OK. I'll wait,' Sam assured him. He steered his mount out of the stable. 'I'll be over by the station.'

Chris nodded and rode back to the saloon.

Once inside he ignored the barkeep, who was busy polishing glasses which he placed on a glass shelf behind the bar. Instead he walked over to the dining table and picked up the coat, which he had, deliberately, left draped over the back of his chair.

'Thought you'd be long gone,' the barkeep remarked as Chris stepped back towards the bar.

'Forgot my coat.' Chris gave an easy grin, holding up the article as though it was a piece of evidence before turning towards the door. Then, as if an afterthought had struck him, he swung around to face the barkeep. 'Never did catch your name.'

'Folks just call me John,' the barkeep offered, innocently. 'Them that asks, anyway.'

Chris clicked his fingers together, then pointed at the man: 'Of course — John Stride. Thought I recognized you.'

The barkeep shook his head and looked away: 'Wrong feller. Name's Rokesby.'

'Well, it was Stride when you did that two-year stretch a while back,' Chris stated, keeping his eyes firmly fixed on the man's face.

'I ain't in the business no more,' John Stride almost whined. 'Kept my hands clean. Once you been in Yuma you don't want to go back.'

'Must've felt good, though,' Chris kept his tone level. 'Talking over old times in here with Liam and the boys.'

'I was surprised to see them,' Stride admitted, throwing the towel down on to the counter. 'And, yeah, I knew what they were plannin'. Swear to God I weren't part of it.'

'You were part of it,' Chris pointed out. 'You did nothing and you said nothing.'

'They were my friends,' Stride protested, unable to look at the deputy.

'Friends?' Chris almost laughed derisively. 'You know as well as I do that if you'd done anything they'd've killed you on the spot.'

'Yeah, I wouldn't've put anything past that Billy Sweet,' Stride had to concede. 'Never took to him then — let alone now. But Liam, he was different — we go back a while.'

'And he ran out on you,' Chris sneered. 'Left you to the mercy of the court. Or have I got it wrong?'

Stride shook his head: 'No, that's how it was. Liam only cared about one thing and that was saving his skin. Sure, we'd done the same to others — but I never thought he'd do it to me.'

'You live and learn,' Chris observed drily.

'You do,' Stride admitted. He picked up the towel and resumed his chores. 'Been here ever since I came out of Yuma. Pay not that good but I like it here.'

'And now that Decker and Sweet are dead?' Chris asked innocently, to cut the reminiscing and get to the point. 'What did Liam want you to do?'

Stride chuckled to himself before giving Chris a straight look.

'You know, you're good, mister,' Stride shook his head as he gave the deputy the credit he was due. 'Send him a telegram. Nothing more. I meant what I said — I don't want any part of that life any more.'

'Well, just make sure you send it,' Chris suggested, with a wink.

'I'll make sure he gets the message,' Stride promised.

'Luck to you.' Chris waved. 'Good to meet up with you, John — Rokesby.'

'And thanks to you,' Stride said gratefully.

Chris felt confident as he turned his back on the barkeep and walked out of the saloon. For the John Stride whom he had known had been a thief and not a killer.

'Took your time,' Sam grumbled when Chris caught up with him. 'So what did Stride have to say for himself?'

'You recognized him too, huh?' Chris

44

scolded, as they took their horses across the tracks. 'And you said nothing.'

'Said I was getting old — not blind,' Sam fired back. 'Come to that, you said nothing, either.'

'Couldn't get a word in edgeways,' Chris reminded him. 'You were too busy going on about Decker and Sweet.'

'Yeah, still can't figure out why they ran at us,' Sam muttered.

'Oh, shut up about it,' Chris yelled at him. 'Is this going to be your sole topic of conversation all the way to Carfax?'

Sam let out a mighty guffaw.

'Had you going there, boy,' he said.

Like hell you did, Chris thought to himself. Sometimes you're just like a dog with a bone. You just can't let go.

'You wait 'til you get to be my age.'

'Your age? Which age? Are we talking fifty now?'

'Let's not get into that again.'

* ★ ★

Pete Gingell stood on the platform and watched the two riders, their banter fading into the distance, as they followed the railtracks north.

Nothing changes with them two, he thought, as he turned to find the barkeep climbing up on to the platform.

'What you doing here?' Gingell demanded, suspiciously, for he found it strange that the man had strayed so far from the saloon.

'Need to use the telegraph,' Stride said, looking up the track. 'I promised a friend.'

Gingell followed his gaze but did not ask the question that started to form in his mind.

'I'll send it,' he said with a sigh.

While Stride dictated Gingell tapped away on the key. His hand did not hesitate, though his curiosity was aroused by what Stride's message contained.

'Like I said,' Stride stated before Gingell could ask a question. 'I did this for a friend.'

Gingell just nodded as he locked the morse key.

3

There was nothing that excited the watcher more than being able to lean his arms on a corral pole and watch a herd of beeves climbing the steeply angled boards into a cattle wagon. There had to be going on for 500 head being shifted. The air resounded with their mooing and the clash of horns as the steers were whipped by sweating, dust-covered cowhands.

Sights, sounds and smells all mingled together. This was his world — a place where men rode herd across the open land to whatever destination. That and the scent of danger that came with the risks of rustling the steers in the first place.

'Times are changin', Liam,' a voice murmured in his ear.

Liam Fogarty turned his stocky body towards the speaker, a slim man, dressed in a light-brown shirt and pants. He had a handsome, tanned face and a shock of fair hair falling from beneath the brim of a grey Stetson. A pair of pale-grey eyes met his gaze.

'Clint,' Liam greeted, a smile curling his lips; a smile that did not reach his small, piglike brown eyes. 'This anything to do with you?'

'Yup, we've just finished shipping over a thousand head,' Clint replied, thinking what an ugly mug Fogarty had. 'Now we can ship east, west or north instead of riding herd and eating dust. All done legal and we get to keep the profits.'

It was the sort of thick face that suggested one of those Irish pugilists that he had heard about. In Fogarty's case there was an element of truth in that he had fought bareknuckle in the illegal matches that took place in the back rooms of New York bars. That was until he killed his first man; then he had come West and found himself a new trade.

Now there was nothing for him here, except the plain stealing of a herd, rebranding before leaving them in the stockyards for shipment. The railroad was changing his way of life and he hated it.

'Pa said to make sure we found you,' Clint continued, leaning his back against the poles and watching the last of the steers board the wagons.

'We?' Liam queried, his eyes on the men as they swung the doors closed and locked them.

'Brother Perry's with me,' Clint supplied, with a wicked glint in his eye. 'Though got to admit he wasn't happy about linkin' up with you again.'

'Still holds a grudge?' Liam spat out the assumption, for he had no liking for having to face Perry Jaeger again.

'You broke his nose,' Clint reminded him.

'And I'll break it again,' Liam promised, his thick lips curving into a snarl. 'If he wants to insult the Irish again then I'll damn well do it. Make fun of me — I can take a joshin' but no one does the Irish down. Understand that?'

Clint Jaeger shrugged: 'Don't concern me. I ain't got a beef with you or the Irish. Just thought I'd warn you.'

Fogarty pushed down on the corral pole and used the momentum to turn around. For a moment he stood there thinking things through. If they were to work together then things would have to be dealt with here and now.

'Where's Perry now?' Liam demanded, without looking at the other Jaeger brother.

'Probably drinking himself sober.' Clint chuckled, coming alongside the Irishman. 'Got hisself drunk last night and once he's on the drink there's no stopping him until you carry him home.'

Liam shook his head, unable to stop himself from laughing.

'Yeah, we've done that many a time,' Liam reminisced, his voice light and even. ' 'Cept he never knew it was my shoulders that carried him. Even that time I busted his nose — it was me who carried him down to the doc's house.'

'Perry don't know about that,' Clint confessed wryly, recalling the incident in his mind. 'If he was told, then he's forgotten about it.'

'Or plain just doesn't want to remember it.' There was bitterness in Liam's tone. 'Still, it don't matter now. We'll just have to settle for our differences and learn to work together again. Don't mean we have to be friends.'

'Just don't expect me to take sides,' Clint warned him.

'Got no expectations,' Liam assured him, clapping him on the shoulder. 'Got something to do. I'll catch up with you.'

Clint shrugged. 'Then you'd best be quick. We're plannin' on leavin' before sundown.'

'Where'll I find you?' Liam asked.

'The Last Chance,' Clint replied. 'It's down the second right side-street

— you can't miss it.'

'I'll be there,' Liam promised and without another word he walked away.

It was good to be on his own again. Sure, he was looking forward to working with some of the old outfit again but it wouldn't be the same. He had been used to running his own gang, and now he would have to learn how to be a part of a team again. It wasn't as if he had been asked to join them for he had been the instigator of the move. He had killed a man and now that he was running from the law he needed a place to hide.

Here no one could touch him. There would be no Wanted notices against him and his pursuers would have no jurisdiction. At least he hoped they wouldn't. Besides, the Jaegers had come this way and no one had taken them in. So he felt certain that he could lose himself, and maybe one day he would be forgotten about.

In all his forty-six years he had killed three men. The first had been an

English bailiff who had tried to evict his father; the next had been a fellow Irishman in a bareknuckle contest — both men had died by his fists and in anger. The result of a weakness of not knowing when to stop. The third had been a man who was trying to stop Fogarty from taking his herd. The shot had meant to scare the man away, force him to duck into hiding. Only he didn't, he died with a bullet through his skull because Liam had misjudged everything in the darkness. He knew that no one would believe him, especially after someone had pointed the finger at him.

When he had heard that the law was looking for him he had no choice but to abandon the herd and make a run for it. Except for Val Decker and Billy Sweet, the rest of the gang didn't want anything to do with him. Liam had been branded a killer and they hadn't wanted their names to be tarnished. There was no doubt in his mind that they had taken the herd to Mexico but that was not his problem.

He was more concerned about Decker and Sweet. He might be going to join friends but he would feel safer amongst them if he knew for certain that he had back-up.

For the umpteenth time he entered the tiny telegraph shack by the station. The telegrapher glanced up but said nothing. Instead, he reached into a pigeon hole beside him and took out an envelope which he dropped on to the narrow shelf that served as a counter in front of him.

'Came in quarter of an hour ago,' the telegrapher told him. 'Hope it's what you're expectin'.'

Liam Fogarty said nothing as he picked up and examined the envelope. Then he turned on his heel, walked out of the office and sat down on the step outside. He ripped open the envelope, which he crumpled and tossed to one side. Then began to read the message.

After a second reading he began to smile. It was a pity that Decker and

Sweet were dead but they were no real loss to Fogarty; he did not mourn their passing, for they had done the job of killing Sam Ward. And he had to admit that he would miss the lawman who had dogged his trail for so long.

At least, or so Liam felt, young Deputy Ford would be more concerned with taking his mentor home than continuing the pursuit. Content with his lot Fogarty screwed up the telegram and tossed it to one side. Time, he decided, for a celebratory drink.

As he walked away from the telegraph office a figure emerged from behind the shack. Head down, he watched Fogarty from the corner of his eye as he stooped to pick up the discarded telegram. He uncrumpled the paper and scanned the message before folding it up and slipping it into the breast pocket of his buckskin jacket.

'You've got a lot of explaining to do, Liam,' he muttered bitterly out loud, as he watched Liam Fogarty disappear down a side turning.

Liam Fogarty stepped into the saloon and allowed time for his eyes to adjust to the dim interior. There was very little light and what there was came from the two large windows at the front and one at the rear. All the glass had a dull, brown coating caused by dust and the heavy tobacco smoke. What little air there was came through the open batwinged doorway. He glanced around until he spotted Clint Jaeger, who was standing by a round table in the far corner, talking to two men. Instantly, Liam grinned with pleasure as he recognized the barrel shape of Ben Buell. They had been good friends back in the old days but had lost touch when Buell had gone on the run.

The other man, a thin runt dressed in shabby, baggy clothing, was a stranger to him. There was something about his relaxed pose that suggested to Liam that this was a dangerous man. It was with caution that he approached the group.

The thin man, as Liam had expected,

had noticed his approach and, though he still appeared at ease, there was an air of alertness about him. His body had shifted a fraction, as had his right hand, which had dropped from the table where he had held a glass, to his lap close to his holstered gun.

'Liam,' Clint greeted enthusiastically as he noticed Fogarty. 'Get your business done?'

Liam nodded, careful to acknowledge Clint while keeping the other man in his vision.

Up close, he looked more like a kid. A fuzz sprouted from his pointed chin and crooked front teeth prevented his mouth from fully closing. Narrow eyes showed no expression as they stared up at Fogarty.

'You don't know Billy, do you?' Clint mentioned, realizing that the kid and Fogarty had never met. 'That's Billy McDonald.'

Liam nodded. Billy McDonald just stared back with those cold, expression-less eyes.

'So what you been up to these last few years?' Ben Buell asked excitedly as Liam sat down next to him.

'This and that.' Liam shrugged, not ready to be that open in present company for he had decided that if there was any catching up to do then it could be done later.

'Killed a man,' Billy McDonald stated, his voice low.

Liam turned slowly to face his accuser, who appeared to be too busy studying his half-full glass of beer. Buell, with a frightened expression on his face, divided his attention between both men. Although a question formed in Buell's mind he was hesitant to ask it. Instead he drew back, content to leave the situation in Clint or McDonald's hands.

'That was an accident,' Liam protested, his mind racing in confusion as he wondered how the kid could know about it.

'Maybe.' The kid shrugged. 'Seems to me that when a man pulls a gun he means to use it.'

'I just wanted to put a scare . . . ' Liam faltered, as he wondered why he was trying to justify his actions to a total stranger.

'You never mentioned this before,' Clint stated, with concern. 'We don't want no trouble here.'

'You won't get none,' Liam countered with sincere intent. 'I can promise you that.'

Clint stabbed a finger at him: 'There had better not be. We don't want the law coming for us — not now. We've all got something good going for us now.'

Liam looked confused.

'We're not in the business any more,' Ben Buell supplied.

'The bad old days are over, Liam,' Clint added. 'Though we are not without problems. There's those that are tryin' to fence us in.'

'And I fit in — where?' Liam asked, suspiciously.

The set-up sounded all wrong to him. It was as though he was hearing something that was not being said. Did they see him just as another gun or were they planning something that required his expertise?

'We're giving you a chance,' Perry Jaeger stated, making his appearance felt. 'Real cattle work. Hope Clint's told you — we're writing ourselves a clean slate.'

Perry had ambled into the saloon not long after Fogarty and had contented himself with being an onlooker in the shadows where he had listened to the men talk. One thing was certain and that was that he had not, as Clint had supposed, been drinking.

Liam turned in his seat with a question forming on his lips.

Perry Jaeger was almost a twin of his brother. The only ways to spot the difference were the shortness of his hair and the fact that his broken nose had been flattened against his face.

'Let me put you in the picture,' Perry continued. He pulled out a chair, which he spun around before sitting straddle-legged with his elbows folded across the backrest. 'Pa's gone legitimate. We've ploughed our money into our own land and cattle. Except there are some folks who think that we top the herd up from time to time at other people's expense. Pa's fixed up some good deals and we've got opposition. No one's backing us — you understand what I'm sayin'?'

Liam nodded.

'So you got something that you want to get off your chest?' Perry innocently asked Liam. 'You appreciate we don't want no more trouble than we already got.'

Liam shook his head. He was determined not to let Perry Jaeger unnerve him. Despite their differences Liam had a lot of respect for him. The best way to tell the difference between the two brothers was that it was the younger, Perry, who weighed things up while Clint would act on impulse.

'And you arrived on your own,' Perry noticed, his conversational tone still light and interested. 'When can we expect Sweet and Decker?'

'They're not coming,' Liam decided to brazen it out. 'They had other things to do.'

'Nothing to do with the law, then?' Perry made the deduction, innocently.

'The law?' Liam questioned, looking for something that he was sure wasn't there.

'Heard tell you killed a man,' Perry mentioned. 'Not hard to reason that the law would be looking for you.'

'Maybe.' Liam shrugged indifferently, then smiled smugly. 'Doesn't look like they found me, does it? I'm here, aren't I?'

Perry Jaeger nodded as though he was ready to accept Liam at face value. He slipped his hand into his pocket, withdrew a coin and tossed it to the Irishman.

'Come on, Liam, go get a beer,' he grinned. 'We're all friends here — aren't we?'

'Guess so.' Liam smiled back,

relieved that he had got through the grilling.

Perry watched as Liam threaded his way towards the bar, then pulled a piece of paper from his shirt pocket.

'Read that,' he suggested firmly. He tossed the telegram towards his brother.

Clint read the message, his mouth hanging open. He turned to his brother while offering the telegram to Ben Buell. With deceptive speed Billy McDonald leapt up and snatched the telegram from Clint's loose grip.

Billy McDonald, stumbling over the words, read the telegram to himself.

'What's it say?' Buell asked in a worried tone.

'Never mind,' Clint snapped back.

'He should know,' McDonald said evenly, before reading the telegram out loud.

'He never said anything about that,' Clint protested, anxious to reassure his brother. 'Not when I spoke to him.'

'You got that right?' Buell said, as though he could not believe that what he had heard was true. 'Sam Ward's dead?'

'That's what it says,' Perry Jaeger confirmed.

'Well, at least we know why the other two aren't coming,' Billy McDonald said ruefully. 'Don't think I want to work with this Fogarty feller. Can't trust a man who's not going to watch my back.'

'Trouble is,' Perry said wistfully, glancing to where the subject of their conversation was propping up the bar, 'there was a time when you could trust him.'

'Except that time — ' Clint jumped in.

'I don't need to be reminded,' Perry cut in curtly. His fingers, in an unconscious gesture, touched his nose. 'It's written all over my face.'

For a moment all four men were silent, lost in their thoughts as they decided what the contents of that telegram meant to them.

'No matter which way you look at it,'

Billy McDonald decided, breaking the pensive mood. 'Some feller gets killed in the back of nowhere — then the law does what's necessary. Kill a lawman and they get to turn over every rock until they hunt the killer down.'

Perry nodded, for the kid had put into words just what he was thinking.

'Ben?' Perry invited.

Buell licked his lips as his eyes flicked nervously from McDonald to Perry. He would have preferred not to be a part of this conversation.

'I don't figure they will,' he said, his voice shaking. 'The law won't be interested in Liam. He weren't there. The way I see it, Val and Billy done what they did off their own backs.'

'You dumb idiot,' McDonald snapped irritably. He turned to glare at Buell. 'They done it off their own backs? Then why did someone telegraph Fogarty about it? Plain to see that he set it up.'

'You ain't got it,' Buell fired back, almost surprising himself at the way he was standing up to the kid. 'The law won't come after Liam. Ward's killers are dead.'

'Ben's got a point,' Perry acknowledged with a nod; his attention was now back on Billy McDonald.

McDonald spread his arms in a gesture of surrender: 'Let's just hope you're right, then. But I can't help but think that Clint must have some thoughts on this.'

Perry looked at his brother with an enquiring lift of his brows.

'We've got a choice,' Clint stated. 'Billy, there, could dispose of Fogarty. Claim any bounty there is on him — or dump him on the trail for someone to find. On the other hand we deliver him to Pa, as we were supposed to do, and leave the decision to him.'

'That's very deep — for you, Clint,' Perry laughed, for his brother was not known for his intellect. 'Only one problem. If we were to kill him then I don't think that there should be seen to be any connection with us.'

'Then let your pa deal with it,' Ben

Buell pleaded, leaning away from Billy McDonald as though expecting to be the target of the kid's anger.

His face showed shocked surprise when McDonald said: 'Guess Ben's right. Your pa's expecting Fogarty — it's his problem.'

'He'll go mad, you know,' Clint pointed out. 'He had no love for Sam Ward — but he had respect.'

'I'll go along with that,' Perry agreed. 'Sam Ward was one damned good lawman. Pa's had a few run-ins with him but he had the beating of him. Trouble is, there's a hell of a lot more who didn't get past Sam Ward.'

'Or that kid who rode with him,' Clint reminded his brother.

Perry nodded: 'Funny that. But you're right. Last few years old Sam had a partner. Wonder what happened to him?'

'We could find out,' Clint pointed out. 'Send a telegram back to that feller.'

Perry glanced at the telegram but

there was no name to reply to. Besides, he reasoned in his mind, there was no point in advertising their curiosity.

'Don't matter who he is.' Perry grimaced. 'He'll be too busy taking his partner's body home.'

'Guess so,' Clint murmured. He glanced over his shoulder to see Fogarty still propping up the bar and talking to a couple of cowhands. 'Just look at him. He hasn't a clue that we know what he's done. Not a care in the world.'

'Yeah,' Perry laughed. 'And that's the way it stays — right, Ben?'

Buell looked nervously into Perry's cold eyes. Just a blink flickered before he stared down at the table where his hands began, out of worry, to play with each other. He had no liking for the situation he found himself in but it was the Jaegers who tolerated him and paid his wages.

'Yes.' He almost whispered his reluctant response, which brought a scowl to Billy McDonald's face.

'And you trust him?' the kid asked Perry.

'I can,' Perry replied, softly. 'Ben has divided loyalties. That's all. He and Liam go back a bit but Ben here can be relied on. Understand?'

'I understand,' McDonald acknowledged, reluctantly and with a distrustful glance at Ben Buell. 'Don't mean that I like it.'

'Don't expect you to.' Perry shrugged as McDonald uncoiled himself from his chair and stood up. 'Just let it go for now.'

'Whatever you say,' McDonald replied easily, his words implying something different. 'Think I'll go for a stroll.'

'Then head for the livery,' Perry suggested. 'We'll join you. Guess it's time we moved on.'

Perry had not realized that he had held his breath as he watched McDonald leave the saloon. With a massive sigh of relief he turned his attention back to Ben, who was still nervously fiddling with his fingers.

'That man is going to get us killed one day,' Buell murmured to the table top.

'Maybe, Ben.' Perry gave a quick, worried glance at his brother, Clint.

'Him or Liam,' Clint responded, levelly. 'Those two aren't going to mix. Maybe you was right in the first place. We drop Liam and tell pa he never showed.'

'Then you do it.'

'Let Billy do it. You know he wants to.'

Perry grinned: 'Sometimes you come up with a good idea.'

'No.' The word was drawn-out and loud and was all the more surprising since the protest came from Ben. 'No, you made a promise. You promised to leave it to your pa. That's what I agreed to.'

'You know something, Ben?' Perry said, leaning on hands spread on the table, his face coming close to Ben's. 'The one thing I've never liked about you is that you can always find a way to prick my conscience.'

Ben dropped his head and folded his fidgeting fingers: 'Then stick with what you promise.'

'I don't break my promises,' Perry assured him, standing up to glance at his brother. 'Never done that before — can't do it now.'

'Yeah,' Clint agreed. 'Let's just go home and get this thing settled once and for all.'

4

Within half a day's ride from Dennett Junction the rough, dusty, scrubland had become a lush landscape of bright-green grass. Open range spread out before them and it was not long before they saw the distant shapes of cattle grazing over to the east of the rutted track that Sam and Chris were following. It would lead, eventually, to the growing town of Carfax.

From time to time cowboys had, out of curiosity, ridden by just to check them out. Sometimes, as they got closer to Carfax they got lucky and found someone who was willing to while away the time of day. Men who talked about cattle, the country and, most important, told them local gossip.

There was a rumour that rustlers were working the ranches up north and to the east of Carfax. So far most of the ranches that they had passed had not apparently seen any trouble. One thing that they did learn was that something was brewing in the direction that they were heading.

'Looks to me as though you're riding into trouble,' Sam observed, as they rode together towards their destination.

'Jaeger and Fogarty,' Chris mused, with a shake of his head. 'Just can't believe that they would head there.'

'No?' Sam queried drily. 'You've held that notion close to you since Carfax got mentioned.'

'Just hoped that it wasn't so,' Chris admitted reluctantly. 'That it'd all turn out to be a coincidence.'

'You can't go in on your own,' Sam protested, attempting to advise his deputy against such a foolhardy notion.

'No choice.' Chris shrugged, unable to look anywhere but at the trail ahead. 'There's Ma to think about. I can't let her down.'

'You'll have no authority,' Sam reminded him, his voice anxious though he knew that the deputy would not do anything stupid. 'What'll you do when you come face to face with Jaeger or Fogarty?'

'That'll be down to them,' Chris replied, his voice firm and even. 'I won't start anything. All I want to do is go visit my father's grave and make sure that Ma's all right.'

'I don't get it,' Sam said, with a worried shake of his head. 'Someone kills your father and you don't seem interested in his killer.'

'That's a matter for the law.' The reply came with cold detachment. 'That's what you taught me, wasn't it? Besides, all that that telegram says is that my pa was killed. There's no saying who did it. So, until I know the facts I can't begin to speculate about what I would do next.' Chris turned to face Sam and smiled grimly. 'Whatever I do it won't be outside the law.'

For a moment Sam stared into those candid eyes, then nodded. Chris, he had to concede, would err on the side of caution as he had always done.

'Yeah, I know,' Sam muttered. 'Just can't help but worry for you.'

This last comment was made as the town of Carfax loomed in the distance. The promise of a cooked meal was enough to spur both men on to drop their conversation and close the distance with as much speed as possible.

The coming of the railway had brought about a building boom. The one-street town that had grown up alongside Henry Carfax's trading post had expanded with new streets built along a grid system. The old trading post was still in the centre of town but was now a double-fronted emporium, which was run by Henry Carfax's grandson. Opposite this building was the red-brick permanence of the law office that Sheriff Tom Carrick shared with Deputy Nate Dawson. Dawson, who topped six two in his socks, was in his mid-thirties and a native of Carfax. His youthful good looks and his natty appearance made people think that he was soft. He always wore white shirts and a grey suit, under which he wore a shoulder rig.

Carrick, who was short and stockier with a preference for range gear, was older by about fifteen years. Between them they policed Carfax and it's surrounds. Both men took their jobs seriously to the point that any attempt at rowdiness was soon quelled. They and their respective deputies policed the town with a no-nonsense approach for which the citizens were grateful. It meant that they could go about their business in peace.

Carrick, sitting in a rocker out front of the law office reading a book, spotted the two riders as they came in to town. It had been a while since he had seen Sam Ward but he recognized him straight off as he reined in in front of the eating-house just across and down from the office. He thought about getting up and going over to convey a greeting while attempting to discover why Ward was in town. Then he decided against it. If it was business then he'd get to know about it sooner or later.

'Nate,' he called out.

'Yup?' Dawson shouted from the office.

'Visitors,' Carrick stated.

There was a moment's silence followed by the steady clack-clack of bootheels as the deputy stepped out of the office and along the boardwalk to stand by the rocker.

'Anyone interesting?' Nate Dawson enquired, his shaded eyes taking in the street scene.

'Sam Ward,' Carrick told him, still watching the two arrivals as they unsheathed their rifles and climbed the steps up to the boardwalk and into the eating-house.

As Chris went inside Sam paused to look down the street. He gave a perceptible nod of his head towards Carrick, then followed his companion into the neat, well-kept interior.

'Off his patch?' Dawson mused, rubbing his chin. 'Must be looking for someone important.'

'My guess it'll be something to do with the Jaeger boys,' Carrick opined, his certainty of his hunch very evident in his tone. 'Time was they operated on Sam's patch. Reckon there's a connection?'

Dawson shrugged, not interested. 'Not our problem. There's no notices on the Jaegers. And they've not caused us any trouble. If that's what Sam Ward's here for he'll not get any help. Not from me, anyway.'

'Well, we'll just have to wait and see,' Carrick suggested, not sharing Dawson's attitude. 'Maybe he's just passing through.'

'Maybe.' Dawson strolled back to the office, only to pause in the doorway, where he turned back. 'Except that if this is the same Sam Ward who you say you rode with one time — I don't think he's just passing through.'

Carrick had to concede that Dawson had a point, though he was not going to let him know that.

★ ★ ★

'We got spotted,' Sam mentioned over a midday meal of beef and potatoes. 'Saw the way the other feller out front of the law office took a good look at us.'

'So?' Chris asked the question that the older man wanted him to ask.

'Tom Carrick,' Sam grinned. 'Knew him a while back when he rode with the Rangers. Good solid feller. Been town marshal here — phew — six, seven years now. If there's anything we need to know he'll know it.'

'You sure he'll talk to us?' Chris asked, shoving his knife and fork neatly across the diameter of his plate. 'We're out of our jurisdiction here.'

'He'll talk,' Sam was confident. 'He won't be able to stop himself. Talking may be his weakness but he wants to know what you know — if you see what I mean.'

'I get what you mean. So let's go.' Chris started to rise but Sam waved him back down.

'No rush,' Sam advised. 'Tom won't be going no place. 'Sides I'm still hungry enough for a piece of apple pie and another cup of coffee.'

'Time's wasting,' Chris pointed out. He was anxious to get as much information that he could so that he knew what he was riding towards.

'Curiosity,' Sam chuckled. 'It'll kill him. That's the key to get him talking. He'll be bursting to tell us what we want to know. First off he'll wonder why we're here; then he'll think about who's been around, and in the end he'll come to the right conclusion and tell all.'

Chris nodded at this explanation but could not help asking: 'You saying he knows Fogarty?'

'Heard of him, possibly,' Sam said. 'But he'll know if any stranger came into town and, possibly, who that stranger may have met up with. My guess is that Fogarty would've met up with someone we know about.'

'That's if Fogarty was here,' Chris

mentioned, not forgetting that the Irishman had bought a ticket for the next station.

'What did Stride say to you?' Sam prompted, after the pretty young waitress had cleared their plates and taken Ward's order for pie and coffee.

Chris leaned back in his chair and stared at the ceiling, his mind playing through the last few words that he had with John Stride. Then smiled and nodded to himself.

'Thanks for reminding me,' he smiled. 'Think I'll go walk off some of that meal we just ate.'

'Good idea,' Sam murmured with a twinkle in his eye. 'Saves me from having to do it. Be interested to know what Stride said.'

'Me too.' Chris said, thinking of the telegram. He stood up and glanced around to see the waitress approaching with a plateful of thick apple pie. 'Looks like you're going to be loosening that belt of yours by the time you've done with that.'

'One of the pleasures of old age,' Sam chuckled, rubbing his belly. 'Loosening a belt and a button after good food.'

'Just don't nap afterwards,' Chris warned playfully.

Sam did not reply for he was now eagerly looking at the hunk of pie that had been placed in front of him.

'Sure I can't tempt you?' the smiling waitress asked, pleasantly.

Chris glanced at her, his face devoid of expression: 'The only apple pie I ever ate was baked by my Ma.'

'I was only bein' friendly,' the waitress commented as she watched Chris leave the eating-house.

'Don't mind him,' Sam reassured her. 'He's got things on his mind. I figure that I can do this pie justice.'

His words fell on deaf ears as the girl wandered, unheedingly, back to her station by the counter.

★　★　★

The telegrapher listened to Chris Ford's request with an expressionless face. The only information that he was prepared to offer was that a man named Fogarty had, indeed, been in to collect a telegram, and — no, he was not prepared to reveal the contents.

' 'Gainst company policy,' the telegrapher stated firmly and with finality.

'And you adhere to that policy?' Chris murmured, his eyes pinning the man to his chair.

'Well,' the telegrapher faltered, trying to look anywhere but at those steely eyes. 'There are exceptions to the rule.'

'How much?' Chris asked.

'Twenty dollars.'

'How much?'

'Ten?'

'Didn't catch that,' Chris said, easily, as he leaned forward so that the badge showed briefly from beneath his coat.

'Five?' the telegrapher asked, hopefully.

'Company policy comes cheap,' Chris mentioned as he handed over a couple of bills in exchange for the pencilled copy that the telegrapher had written down.

Leaning against the wooden office wall he read the message and was grinning all over his face when he handed the pad back.

By the time he returned to the eating-house Sam was leaning back in his chair, his belt unbuckled and snoring his head off. It seemed to Chris a shame to wake him, so he pulled the vacant chair around and sat next to him.

'This is going to be like waking the dead,' he said out loud and to no one in particular.

'Ain't asleep,' Sam grunted. 'Just resting my eyes.'

'Then your eyes were making funny noises,' Chris commented.

'So what did you find out?' Sam asked, ignoring the sarcastic comment.

'Fogarty got off the train here,' Chris supplied; then, as an afterthought: 'Oh, and by the way, you're dead.'

'I'm what?' Sam jolted upright so fast that he made Chris jump.

'Decker and Sweet succeeded in killing you,' Chris confirmed.

'Damn nerve,' Ward grumbled, hastily buckling his belt back up. 'That's just wishful thinking.'

'Yeah,' Chris chuckled as a new thought struck him. 'And Fogarty'll believe it. Bet you that, right now, he's sure that there's no one on his trail. He'll not have a care in the world.'

'Well, he's going to get one hell of a rude awakening,' Sam promised as he stood up, ready to leave and head for the law office. 'Now, let's get some answers to my questions. I can't wait to see Fogarty's face when I show up.'

Chris wanted to grab Sam's arm and put some reason into him. Then pulled back as he realized that this was not the time or the place to remind Sam that he had no place to go. Suddenly, as a thought struck him, Sam turned to Chris.

'Did you put Stride up to that?' he

asked, suspiciously.

Chris shook his head: 'Must've thought it up himself.'

'Hmm!' Sam grumbled with disbelief as he headed towards the door.

5

'Well, well,' Tom Carrick chuckled as Sam strode into the double-fronted law office.

'Dead man walkin',' Dawson could not help but add.

Sam Ward glanced from one to the other. Both men were seated with their feet propped up on the tops of their respective desks, which were situated opposite each other on either side of the doorway.

'News travels fast,' Sam grumbled. 'How'd you find out about that?'

'It's all around town,' Dawson said coolly. 'Common knowledge, I'd say.'

'Didn't have to pay for it neither,' Carrick pointed out, with a wink in Chris's direction.

Only Chris wasn't listening, for he was too busy staring out of the window as though more content with watching something that was going on outside.

'Guess you're here about the Jaeger boys,' Carrick assumed, giving Sam an enquiring look.

'As if you didn't know,' Sam admitted grudgingly before adding: ''Cept we've not got much interest in them.'

Carrick looked perplexed for a moment, then gave a knowing smile as though he'd already guessed what was the main interest for the new arrivals' presence.

'You mean the feller that got off the train?' Carrick asked, innocently.

'We do that, you know,' Dawson stated in a matter-of-fact tone. 'Train comes in and we check who gets on and who gets off.'

'Gives us an idea of people's coming and goings,' Carrick added.

Tired of the game Sam deliberately gave a description of Liam Fogarty and waited for either man to speak.

'Yep,' Dawson supplied, eventually.

'Rode out with the Jaegers,' Carrick confirmed.

'Do you know where they went?' Sam enquired.

'Stanton,' Dawson replied.

'Then I'd appreciate some help from you.' Sam became businesslike as he turned his attention to the sheriff. 'Fogarty's wanted for murder and I want him brought in.'

Dawson shook his head: 'Can't help you. Stanton's outside the county line.'

'Since when?' Sam demanded.

Lazily, Dawson swung his legs off the desk to the floor and stood up. He turned to face a large map behind his desk.

'I'll show you,' he offered, beckoning Sam over. 'See this red line here?' He pointed out the perpendicular line on the map as Sam stood at his shoulder. 'That's both the county and state border. And this black dot right there under the line is Stanton. Now, and this has come down from the state governor himself, we got no business going into

Stanton. According to this map Stanton should be in your jurisdiction, except that your governor, just as you believe, says that that town is on our side. You see my predicament? Your best chance is to go talk to the sheriff of Stanton — not that he's going to be disposed to hand over your killer to you.'

'Why should he be uncooperative?' Sam asked.

'Matt Jaeger's the law in Stanton,' Tom Carrick supplied before Dawson could respond.

'Self-styled law,' Dawson pointed out, throwing Carrick a black look. 'He just took over after Tom Ford got gunned down.'

'Tom Ford?' Sam queried, stopping himself from glancing back to where Chris was still gazing out of the window.

'Ford was Stanton's sheriff,' Dawson continued, as he perched his bottom on the corner of his desk. 'Well, just during the last couple of years, from about the time Jaeger and his crew turned up.

They took over the old Stanton spread. There's a feller called Aldo Lund who's the figure-head but most folks believe that it was bought with Jaeger's money. First spring round-up produced a lot of problems. Porter Coleman, who owns the neighbouring spread, claimed that the Jaegers seemed to have more calves and unbranded stock than anyone else. He got Tom Ford to go out and inspect the herd. Naturally, Ford couldn't tell who was right or wrong but he managed to calm Coleman down.

'Then there was a ruckus down at the saloon. The loss of their stock was still rankling with Coleman's boys, and they thought they'd take it out on Jaeger's hands. Ford broke up the fight and sent the Jaeger hands home but put two of Coleman's hands in jail for the night.'

'Bit one-sided, that,' Sam commented.

'Not really,' Dawson replied. 'The two men had started the trouble in the first place. They were the ones who had thrown the first punch. From what I heard the Jaegers refused to rise to the bait — just went about their business and let the taunts and jibes simply fly over their heads.

'Anyways, Coleman lost about fifty head — or so he claimed. Ford went out to see the Jaegers, had a talk with them and couldn't find any evidence that that Coleman stock was on Jaeger land. Upshot of that is that Coleman thinks that Ford is in pay of the Jaegers. So, he came to me. Like Ford, I couldn't find anything to back up Coleman's claim. Though, later Tom Chenery found forty-odd head of Coleman cattle wandering on his land. To be honest there's a lot of open range out there and cattle will wander.

'Coleman's answer was to wire off his boundary with the Jaegers — just fenced them in. Jaeger protested but accepted that Coleman could do what he damned well like on his land.

'The real crunch came when Lund brokered a deal with some big concern up north. After Jaeger had brought in the first shipment I had Coleman in my office, shouting the odds with a claim that it was his beef that was being loaded on the wagons. Again, I took a looksee and I couldn't find a thing wrong. At which point Coleman demanded to know how much Jaeger was paying me to look the other way.'

'Was he paying you?' Sam asked, suspiciously.

'Nobody buys me,' Dawson snapped back with fire in his eyes, indignant that anyone should make such an accusation. 'Ford may have taken money — but I can't be bought.'

'But you think Ford did?' Sam questioned, sensing that Chris had stiffened behind him and hoped that he would do nothing stupid.

'Who knows?' Dawson shrugged. 'But he did favour the Jaeger side of things. They could be a rowdy bunch. Shoot a few holes in the sky when they had a few drinks — who doesn't? But tension was high between the Jaegers and the Coleman crew. In the end Ford laid it down the line: Coleman men came in on a Friday night and Jaeger's on the Saturday night.'

'Seemed a fair decision,' Carrick chimed in. 'If I was in the same position I'd've done the same.'

'Only worked for a while,' Dawson told him. 'Then came that Saturday night. A bunch of Coleman's men came into town. The story I got was that they had been out rounding up some strays and missed out on their Friday night. Tom Ford saw them and shepherded them out of the saloon. A lot of angry retorts were thrown at him and he posted them out of town. As they were riding out Ford returned to the saloon. As he came through the door a shot rang out and Ford was killed instantly.'

'One of Coleman's men must've come back,' Sam deduced.

'Or it was Billy McDonald?' Dawson suggested. 'He had his gun drawn — but most of the witnesses say it must've been a reflex action at the sound of the gunshot. Trouble is too many people were ducking for cover to be sure — but they swear blind that McDonald wasn't Ford's killer.'

'And now Matt Jaeger is the law there,' Sam said, thoughtfully. 'Maybe, folks are just too damn scared to name the killer.'

'That thought did cross my mind,' Dawson agreed. 'But it's not my problem — not while Stanton is stuck in the middle of a border dispute.'

'There's another problem, Sam,' Carrick mentioned, anxious to be an authoritative part of the conversation. 'Jaeger's barred all Colemen men from town. If they want supplies they have to come here. This has riled Coleman up so much that he's getting together with other ranchers to put an end to the Jaegers once and for all.'

'I don't think you'll have much luck prising Fogarty out of that mess,' Dawson confided.

'I figure you're right at that,' Sam conceded. 'There's not a lot more I can do, is there?'

'Sorry we couldn't help.' Dawson's apology sounded genuine.

'Well, I guess I'll head home.' Sam sighed, then glanced at Chris. 'You comin', or you just goin' to stand there watching the girls go by all day?'

Dawson waited until Sam and his deputy were across the street before commenting: 'Dumb-ass kid.'

'You reckon?' Carrick asked. 'I'd bet you everything you got that that dumb-ass kid took in everything you said.'

'Yeah?' Dawson responded with a sneer as he settled back into his chair. 'What makes you think that?'

'Just a hunch,' Carrick mused. 'Just a hunch.'

★　★　★

'I can't let you go,' Sam tried to sound authoritative as they walked along the boardwalk opposite the law office. 'You're ridin' into the middle of a range war.'

'I think I might have gathered that,' Chris replied, angrily. 'But I'm not letting Ma down.'

'Oh! Hell,' Sam surrendered. 'Do what you must — just don't get yourself killed. And keep away from Fogarty 'til I've figured out a way to deal with him.'

'Wasn't my intention,' Chris chided. 'Besides, this is where we agreed that I would quit and each of us would go his own way.'

Sam nodded: 'Well, I'll hang around here for a while. Need to sort out things — you know what I mean?'

'Yeah.' Chris nodded, a grin on his face as he clapped the older man on the shoulder.

Sam Ward watched as Chris walked to where they had tethered their horses, but did not wait for his now ex-deputy to mount up. Instead, he turned into the nearby saloon where he intended to forget about his troubles for a while.

6

It was strange to be riding alone without anyone to talk to. It was as though Chris was suffering a physical loss, for he truly missed Sam's company. But then, he reasoned, only he of the two of them could ride into Stanton for a legitimate reason.

Nor was it an easy ride, for many conversations still swirled around in his head as he tried to make some sense from the things that he had heard.

He could not understand how any man could accuse his father of accepting bribes. For all his faults, Tom Ford had always been an honest man who had dealt fairly with other men. Certainly, it could be reasoned that, the way the sheriff of Stanton had dealt with things, it could look a bit suspicious. If there was a fault in that then it was that the man in charge, being a creature of habit, would have dealt with the trouble-causers before he attended to others.

The biggest question that rooted itself into Chris's mind was: why had his father taken on the job in the first place? Tom Ford was a good carpenter and was never without work of some kind — unless there had been a need for some extra regular income.

Until he reached Stanton, he knew that he would not find the answers.

So he followed the old trail that cut its way through the open range until he reached a line of pole fencing that was broken by an open gateway. Here he paused to stare at the sign that swung overhead in the gentle breeze. A sign that proclaimed that PC territory lay beyond the boundary line. His attention was drawn to five riders, approaching from different directions — all, presumably, curious about the stranger that was riding towards town. This told Chris something about Porter Coleman and the lengths that he was prepared to go to protect his cattle.

Later, the long line of barbed-wire fencing that stretched to the horizon seemed to confirm his original assessment. Between the Coleman ranch and town stretched the spread that had once been owned by a man called Arch Stanton. Stanton had been killed during the Civil War and the ranch was taken over by his son, who was not as successful. He was curious to know how it had come into Jaeger's hands and was determined to find that out sometime while he was in town. Stanton itself had hardly changed in the few years he had been away. The main street sat on an uphill curve with just a handful of stores, a saloon, a law office, livery stable and a blacksmith's shop.

The stable and the blacksmith's were the first two buildings he came to as he entered town. Opposite there was a new structure being built — just a timber frame with a rough boardwalk along part of the frontage.

A man sat on a barrel, in what would

be the doorway, drinking steaming coffee while reading a thin book. One of the other builders stopped measuring a plank of wood to pass a comment as he watched the stranger ride up the street. Both men were joined by others and speculation began to pass between them as the rider halted outside the general store.

They watched him hitch his horse to the pole and climb up on to the boardwalk, where he stopped and turned around.

At this moment a six-foot-three 200-pound figure emerged from the law office opposite. He wore a grey shirt, the sleeves of which were rolled halfway up his forearms. A black leather vest hung open above his faded black denim pants, which were tucked into dark riding-boots. His craggy features were exposed by shoulder-length grey hair that had been pulled back and tied in a ponytail. A long grey goatee curved down from his square chin.

Through narrow, dark, slitted eyes he

looked at the man standing on the opposite side of the road. Not that there was much to see, for the brim of the stranger's hat was so low that most of his face was in shadow. But it was the red plaid coat that jogged a vague memory — enough to make him stiffen.

A tiny flicker of a smile passed across the stranger's lips before he turned around to enter the store.

For a moment Matt Jaeger was tempted to cross the street. Then changed his mind, deciding that it was best to leave things to work their way through. Although he was aware that trouble had come to town he was not yet prepared to confront it until he knew how it was going to affect him.

Chris strolled into the store without checking what Jaeger was doing. It was enough that the man knew that he was here and that the next move belonged to him. For now his attention was on Fred Harris, the storekeeper, who was still busy filling the gaps in his shelves, unaware that he had a customer.

'So how come Jaeger's the law here?' Chris asked, announcing his presence, and coming straight to the point.

Taken by surprise the slightly built, balding storekeeper dropped the cans he was holding and turned to face his customer. The remainder of the cans he put hastily on to the counter as he rushed to grasp Chris's hand.

'Good to see you, Chris,' he grinned. 'Didn't know if you'd come back. Figured after what happened — '

'Still my Pa,' Chris reminded him pleasantly. 'And that's in the past. More interested in the present.'

The storekeeper nodded as he cast a furtive glance towards the empty doorway opposite.

'Jaeger's not official,' he explained. 'It's just that after your pa died — well, no one wanted the job.'

'Pa did,' Chris pointed out. 'Don't sound like him but Pa did.'

'That was back when all the trouble started,' Fred explained, fiddling with his apron. 'Frank Burrows couldn't handle those Jaeger hands. A real bunch of hellions they were when they first came here. Anyway, Burrows just ran away and your pa stepped in.'

Chris remembered Frank Burrows as a good lawman but one who had never had to deal with real trouble. So the fact that he had left town came as little surprise.

'I'll be back tonight,' Chris promised. 'Just make sure you got the town council here.'

'Why?' asked a perplexed store-keeper, suddenly aware of a coldness that had seeped into Chris's tone.

For an answer Chris pulled his coat open so that Fred could see the badge.

'This means nothing here,' Chris explained. 'I need one that does.'

'Do you think that's wise?' Fred asked with concern. 'Whoever shot your pa might come gunning for you.'

'Let's hope so,' Chris replied. 'Save me the problem of finding him myself.'

'Chris, I won't . . . ' Fred blurted out, intending to deny the younger man the benefit of hunting revenge from behind the badge.

Instead he was met by a steely look that he had only seen once before. He shuddered as he remembered that day when the boy, half-naked and bleeding from lash marks on his back, had come down the main street. He had called out Tom Ford's name. The man had turned to face his son who had roared out those hate-filled words — that was the last time that Tom Ford had laughed.

Fred snapped back to the present and realized that he had little choice in the matter.

'We'll be here, Chris,' he promised.

Chris nodded. He left the store and stood on the boardwalk, staring up the street. Now that he was here he found it difficult to continue up the street to the white, timber-framed house that had once been his home. Instead he walked up to the Gun Tavern where an old and trusted friend, Joe, was sweeping out the previous night's sawdust into a barrel wedged against the boardwalk.

Joe was in his mid-forties but age had not seemed to touch the youthfulness of his face. He wore his dark hair long so that it framed the lightly tanned skin. High cheekbones gave a hint of his parentage, while piercing blue eyes dared anyone to mention it.

He was dressed, as always, in grey clothes and was as slim now as the day he had drifted into town to become Tom Ford's apprentice and, despite the age difference, Chris's friend.

'Joe,' Chris greeted, waiting for the man to look around.

Slowly, Joe turned around before allowing a big, white-toothed grin to split his tanned features.

'Hey, kid,' he greeted, wrapping his arms around Chris. 'Hell, it's good to see you.' He pulled back to give the younger man a good looking-over. 'You've filled out some.'

'Well, you ain't changed.' Chris grinned.

Joe jerked his head to one side:

'Come on in and I'll get you a drink.'

'Coffee,' Chris suggested, following his old friend into the saloon. 'Won't do for me to go home smelling of beer.'

'Help yourself,' Joe pointed at the pot bubbling away on the top of the stove set in the centre of the room. 'Guess you'll want to know how your pa died.'

Chris went behind the long mahogany bar that ran along one wall and grabbed a mug from beneath the counter.

'Not really,' he answered as he re-emerged to cross the floor to the stove. 'Heard a version already.'

'Well, it wasn't the kid — McDonald,' Joe confirmed, while Chris filled his mug and put the pot back on the stove.

'You sound sure,' Chris said with just enough cynicism in his tone to prompt a response.

'No smoke,' Joe responded, surprised that his word had been doubted. 'No powder smell either.'

'Figured.' Chris shrugged. 'That's the

way I heard it. So, who'd really want to kill Pa?'

Joe looked thoughtful for a moment then asked: 'You really want to know? Then anyone — for any number of reasons.'

'You got a for instance?' Chris prompted, after taking a sip of coffee.

'Just things folks said,' Joe stated, trying hard to remain neutral.

'You think that the Jaegers had him in his pocket?'

'I don't believe it,' Joe admitted. 'After all, Jaeger's the law here now.'

'Just goes to show.' Chris chuckled as he poured himself another cup of coffee. 'There are two ways of looking at a backhander.'

'None of my business really,' Joe pointed out as he hefted up the barrel full of last night's sawdust and walked to the back of the saloon.

Chris, carrying his cup of coffee, followed his friend out back to where Joe was emptying the barrel on to a pile of embers. He squatted down on his haunches as Joe fanned the embers, and watched as the flames took hold, sending up a cloud of grey smoke.

'I quit,' Joe said, keeping his back to the listener. 'The day you rode away. Your pa was looking for a scapegoat — and it wasn't going to be me.'

'You did nothing wrong,' Chris pointed out.

Joe whirled around, his eyes narrowed: 'Didn't I? I taught you how to fight — but I never expected — '

'No one did,' Chris explained, trying to calm the other man's anger. 'Not even me. All I ever wanted was to know how to defend myself. I wanted . . . '

Chris faltered. He could not say the words out loud but the real reason lay in the fact that he had wanted his pa to be proud of him. The years of taunts about his size; about how Charlie and Hal were men compared to him and how they had inherited their father's skills. But the most damaging humiliation was that his father denied him by saying that he could not have fathered such a child. All the things that he would rather have forgotten rose to the edges of his memory, fuelling his anger. Suddenly he stood up and handed the empty cup to Joe.

'I never meant for you to get blamed,' Chris stated. Then he turned on his heel and walked back through the saloon.

By the time he had reached and mounted his horse Chris was feeling a lot calmer. What lay in the past should have stayed there and maybe, he reasoned, coming home had been a mistake. But he was a lawman first and foremost, which meant that he had a job to finish by bringing Liam Fogarty in. Also, if he could, to make sure that his father's killer met with the justice he deserved.

7

The cemetery lay at the top of the hill just past Tom Ford's workshop and lumber yard, no great distance for a coffin to travel to its final resting place. Though there were not many graves — certainly not more than fifty, all placed in neat rows.

Tom Ford's grave, placed close to the fence within a stone's throw of his workshop, was the newest. New shoots of grass had begun to sprout through the mound as though delivering the message that life carried on doing what it did naturally. A piece of wood, neatly carved with the name and age of the deceased, served as a headstone.

With reverence Chris reached out to touch the smooth carving that could have only been done by someone with a skilled touch. Whoever had etched the words had done his father proud.

'Say your piece and move on,' a rough, gravely voice barked from behind him. 'There's nothin' for you here.'

Chris stiffened, fought down the sudden burst of anger that would have led him to doing something that he would regret. Instead, he slowly rose to his feet and took his time before turning from the grave to face his brother.

Charlie Ford was the spit of his father. Six four and broad-shouldered. He had a well-muscled frame and his stance suggested that he was ready for a fight. As did his rugged-featured face, the thin lips curved in a grimace while pure hatred smouldered in his dark narrow eyes. As his hawk nose twitched with disgust, he wiped the sleeve of his green-checked shirt under his nostrils as though wiping away a foul odour.

'Just get on your horse and ride.' Charlie spat the words out as though they were bullets.

'Can't do that,' Chris replied evenly,

not rising to the bait. 'Hate to disappoint Ma.'

'She won't be disappointed,' Charlie sneered. 'She'll be damned glad you never showed.'

'That's not what Ma says.' Chris was trying hard to keep his emotions under control, for he neither wanted to do or say anything that would evoke a violent reaction. 'Got a telegram from her asking me to come.'

This piece of information took Charlie Ford off-balance. His thick eyebrows lowered over his confused eyes. Quickly, he recovered from the shock and lurched forward to grab Chris's right arm in a firm grip.

'Don't see as how that's possible,' he growled out a warning. 'But figurin' that to be true you'd best have your say and then move on.'

'I'll be around for a while,' Chris warned, breaking free of the grip. 'I want Pa's killer standing trial.'

Charlie shook his head: 'There'll be no trial. You go play lawman someplace else because I intend to deal with Pa's killer myself.'

'And just who do you figure killed Pa?' Chris asked, innocently.

'You did,' Charlie exploded, thrusting his face into that of Chris. 'Pa never lived down that day. That's why he took the badge to prove he was a better man than you. You just ain't got any idea of what you done.'

Chris allowed himself a slight smile as he said: 'And you had nothing to do with it, did you? I suppose it wasn't you who left the workshop unlocked. It wasn't you who had Laurie Paine in there with you that night. What I do know is that it wasn't you that got the whipping. I locked up that night, just as Pa asked, and you knew that. But you said nothing — you just let the ball start rolling. It's the story of your life, Charlie — everything is anyone else's fault but yours.'

The words struck deep, for Charlie's face reddened and his big hands bunched into fists. For a moment his mouth moved but no sound came out.

'Any time, brother,' Chris offered. 'Here and now — or whenever you think you feel the need.'

'Just get the hell away from me,' Charlie growled. 'You've seen Pa's grave. Say what you need to Ma — then you git. By sundown I want to see you ridin' down that street, or you'll have regrets.'

Chris just nodded before stepping back a pace so that he could walk around both the grave and his brother. Not once did he turn his back, for he expected a cowardly attack at any moment. Instead, Charlie just stood there with a feeling of impotence as he watched Chris walk slowly towards the house.

For a while Chris just stood in the shadow of the porch. He barely noticed Charlie stride past, giving the house a wide berth as he made his way down the main street. Chris was more concerned about how things would work out once he entered the house. He had always been protective of his mother but he had walked away five years before and, until now, had not returned. There had been letters home but there had not been replies. After a few months he had given up and got on with his new life.

Had his mother not asked him to come home he would not have bothered. Then again, he reasoned, his sense of justice would have brought him back, considering the way his father had died.

Slowly, he gripped the doorknob and gave it a twist before pushing the door open. For a moment he stood, framed, on the threshold while his eyes looked beyond the staircase to the half-open kitchen door at the end of the hall. He closed his eyes while he allowed the aroma of baking bread to assail his nostrils. It was that lingering smell that told him that he was home.

He closed the door gently before walking down the hallway and peering through the door. He allowed himself a slight smile as he watched his mother, her arms covered to the elbows in flour, as she mixed a fresh bowl of pastry.

In front of her was a pan filled to the brim with water and, as she rolled the pastry, it rippled sending slices of apple bobbing across the surface. Already, Chris could taste the pastry that would melt in his mouth and blend with the hot, softened apples.

A scrape of a chair on the stone floor wiped the smile from his face and alerted him to the fact that there was someone else in the house. This was confirmed as the door opened wider with an abruptness that made him step back a pace.

'Oh, my God,' his brother Hal barked, also backing away as recognition overtook the sudden shock of finding someone in the house. 'Chris — you sure got a way with makin' an appearance.'

'Hal.' Chris nodded cautiously, not sure that his brother's greeting was genuine. 'Good to see you.'

But Hal wasn't listening. He was too busy calling to their ma who, despite her shortness of stature, shouldered her tall son to one side. She almost leapt at Chris as her arms looped around him, holding him tight and sending up showers of flour that clung to the back of his red plaid coat.

'Ma,' he gasped. 'Sorry, but — '

'You're here,' she half-sobbed into his shoulder. 'That's all that matters.'

After a few minutes she let him go and stood back to appraise him. 'Well, you've filled out some.' She nodded with approval. 'And you've got shot of that paleness you had.'

'You know how it is,' Chris looked a little abashed.

'Damned if I do.' Hannah Ford shook her head, while her eyes looked on him with pride. 'Least you made something of yourself — like Hal here.'

'And Charlie,' Chris reminded her.

'Charlie?' Hal grimaced. 'Charlie ain't done a thing.'

'I thought he joined the army,' Chris

119

said, suddenly aware that he might have got the wrong idea.

'Yeah, he did,' Hal confirmed.

'Spent most of his time in prison.' Their mother almost spat the words out.

'Hit an officer — well, that's what I heard,' Hal chimed in, anxious to be a part of the conversation. At this Chris started laughing.

'It's not funny,' his ma scolded, trying to suppress her own laughter.

'I bet he didn't want to do what he was told,' Chris chuckled.

'You'd win,' Hal guffawed.

'It's tragic, really,' Chris stated, sobering up and seeing the serious side of his elder brother's actions.

At which point Hannah Ford took charge of the situation by shepherding her two sons out of the hall back into the kitchen. From force of habit they sat at the table while their mother went to top up two mugs with steaming coffee, which she set down in front of them. Then she stood back with a look of admiration on her face. At least they were getting on and bringing a little harmony into her house. It was best, she believed, to savour the moment for she was aware that a storm lay on the horizon and that it was essential that Chris and Hal should bond together.

Even though they conversed Chris was guarded for he was well aware that Hal and Charlie had ganged up against him in the past.

'Don't blame you none,' Hal offered, broaching the subject that lay between them, 'for what happened between you and pa.'

'It's done with,' Chris answered cautiously, his shrewd eyes on his brother.

'Not if it stands between us.'

'Only if you let it,' Chris slid his chair back and stood up. He removed his coat and draped it across the back of his chair.

Hal stared at the badge pinned to his brother's vest.

'So it's true,' he remarked. 'Charlie said — '

'I can guess,' Chris said curtly. He sat down.

'Laurie told us all about what happened that night,' Hal continued, anxious to get the explanation in. ''Cept she told us that it weren't the only time that Charlie got you in to trouble with pa.'

'And?' Chris prompted, waiting to see what was coming next.

'I guess I was wrong,' Hal said, his apology drifting towards a point just above Chris's head. 'Should never have believed a word that Charlie said. Should never have sided with him — not when we were kids.'

Chris allowed a silence to hang between them, not to make Hal feel uncomfortable, but so that he could assess the situation, for Hal had used this tactic before. In the past he had tried to lull Chris into a false sense of amicability that Chris had never allowed himself to feel since he left home. There was this history to consider before he could feel confident that now things were different.

'Hal,' he murmured, 'I'd like to believe you. But we've been here before and I can't take your word on this. Guess from now on it's what you do and say that's going to heal things between us.' He glanced up at his mother who was standing, stiff-backed by the stove, having just slid the apple pie in to cook. 'Sorry, Ma, but it's the best I can offer.'

Slowly, she turned around and gave both boys a weak smile: 'Time will tell.'

There was something ominous in those three words but Chris chose not to challenge the warning. Instead, he began to regret his decision to return home. It would have been easy for him to decide that it was already time for him to move on. He had seen Ma and visited his father's grave, which should have been enough. Charlie had shown that he did not want his younger brother around, while Hal had done nothing to prove his trust. Therefore, it would have been easier to ride on with no regrets except that his father's killer would be allowed to walk free. Chris's sense of justice would not allow that.

'Want for me to take your horse down the livery for you?' Hal volunteered unexpectedly.

Chris shrugged: 'If that's what you want to do.'

Seemingly glad that he had something to do, Hal hastened to put on his coat and run outside.

'Sit down, Chris,' Hannah Ford commanded; though her tone was soft, it was authoritative. Chris did as he was told as his mother sat at the head of the table.

'Before you ask,' she continued, without waiting for him to make himself comfortable. 'I don't know who killed your father. But I want you to find him.'

'Intended to do that,' Chris assured her, giving her a determined look.

'Really?' his mother was surprised by

his response. 'You looked like you was getting ready to run again.'

'Didn't run the last time,' he grinned. 'Just walked away. Walked all the way to the livery and never looked back.'

'With no regrets?' his mother demanded, leaning forward in her chair as though to watch his reaction more closely.

'None, Ma,' he said, sincerely. 'I'd had enough. I'd taken enough.'

'You could've talked to me,' she pointed out.

'About what?' Chris tried to fight the fierceness in his tone. 'You were loyal to Pa. And Charlie could do no wrong — you was always making excuses for him.'

'He was my first-born,' she argued, weakly.

'So — what is the point of this conversation?' Chris forced an issue which, he could see, was making her squirm. 'You want to tell me that I'm the bad son? You want me to feel guilty because I could take it no longer and beat down my own father?'

'Guilty?' she yelled, stopping his tirade. Then she calmed down. 'That's the one thing that your father didn't want you to feel. That day he came home — he was not looking for you but asking for you. I thought that he would be in a bad mood — we all kept out of his way. None of us knew which one would feel the backlash. Then, when we were alone, he just said that he had never seen the like. Who'd've guessed, he said, that it would be the runt who proved to be able to stand up for himself?'

This admission caused Chris a lot of confusion. Although he could not disbelieve his mother he could not see his father admitting to anything good about his middle son.

Chris shook his head: 'Sorry, Ma, but that ain't my father speaking. I took him down in the street and shamed him in front of all those who respected him. He'd not come home and say anything like that.'

'Your father respected those who stood up to him,' Hannah assured him. 'Just as much as he had respect for those who stood beside him.' She stood up, walked around the table and came to sit beside him, laying her hands on his. 'He was proud of you — prouder than you'll ever know.'

Chris shook his head. 'Did it have to come to that to make him proud of me?'

Hannah nodded her head: 'Yes, Chris, I think you did have to tackle the problem head on. Oh, Charlie had his scrapes and leaned on your pa to get him out of trouble. More often than not he'd drag Hal into more trouble than he could handle. But you — you were always different. But your pa never hated you.'

'Always being called the runt.' Chris allowed bitterness to colour his tone. 'Put down because I liked to read — to learn while being unable to — '

'Chris — that's done with,' Hannah scolded, gripping his hand. 'It's in the past. Let it lie there. You can't let it gnaw at you or it'll destroy the man you've become. Think on this — why did you come back?'

'Because you asked me to,' Chris said simply, lifting his head to look her in the eyes. 'I didn't want to come — but, Ma, it took you five years to do that. All the letters I wrote..'

Hannah nodded ruefully: 'I know. I didn't reply — I thought that if I did I'd just make matters worse for you.'

Abruptly, he pulled his hand from hers and stood up. It was all too much for him to take in and all he wanted to do was get away from the situation. Families, he thought, who really needs them? Mothers, fathers and brothers all out to manipulate a person and mould that person into who they wanted him to be. All demanding a loyalty that should just come naturally. Instead, Chris had become his own man who had now found that he owed nobody anything.

Without a word of explanation he left

the kitchen and walked along the hall. He paused at the foot of the stairs where he picked up his saddle-bag, which Hal presumably had left there and hefted it up over his shoulder. He climbed the stairs, entered the back bedroom and glanced around.

Nothing had really changed. A set of bunks stood against one wall while a single one lay against the wall opposite. In between was a low dresser with a blue chipped bowl and jug on top; alongside were two hairbrushes and two cut-throat razors. The top bunk bed, like the single one, was neatly made while the lower bunk was unmade with clothes strewn across the bottom, some of which had made it to the floor. This marked the difference between Hal and Charlie. Showed, also, that this room had not been the childhood sanctuary that he had once believed it to be.

Hal and Charlie together on the one side and he, alone, on the other. And in the dark his brothers would make their taunts while his parents lay in their bed and did nothing.

At least, Chris mused, no one had attempted to take over his space. His bed, with the shelf above loaded with books, was as he had left it. He reached up and snatched down the first book to hand — a copy of one of Beadle's dime novels about Jesse James. In an instant he recalled his father, in a lighter mood, giving him the book and joking that he was lucky to get a copy. Though to this day he never knew why.

He flopped down on to his bed and lay back, opened the book and began to read. He had hardly reached the bottom of the page before he fell asleep, the book falling open on his chest.

8

Night was falling on Carfax when Sam Ward left the eating-house and made his way across to the saloon on Main Street. He had spent the past couple of nights visiting two of the town's saloons, where he had sat at a table and nursed a few beers while listening into other folk's conversations. For the most part it was general gossip and easy to dismiss; then, familiar names would come up. At this Sam became alert, without showing it, as he listened intently. Unless he was part of the conversation he did not intrude but stored the information away to be saved for a time when he could seek an answer.

In this he was unlike Chris. Chris would amble into other people's lives and by the time he was done he would know a darn sight more and leave folks thinking that they had just met up with a long-lost friend.

What Sam had heard along the way served more to confirm what he already knew. Except that there seemed to be a 'but' beginning to emerge. The more he thought about it the more convinced he was that there was an underlying story that had only been vaguely hinted at.

'No home to go to?' a familiar voice asked. There came a creak of a chair as someone sat down beside him. 'Not sent your boy to get Fogarty, have you?'

'Hell's teeth,' Sam grumbled at the newcomer, Tom Carrick. 'Creepin' up on a man like that could get you killed.'

'And a noose round yer neck to boot.' Carrick grinned, though his eyes didn't reflect humour as he studied his man. 'The boy? Where is he?'

Sam sighed and played with his glass, creating wet circles on the table top. Seemingly distracted he debated with himself just how much he should disclose.

'Not to get Fogarty,' Sam said,

huffily. 'He's got business of his own to sort out.'

'In Stanton?' Carrick chuckled with disbelief. 'Saw him ride out and that road leads to only one place.'

'Tom,' Sam snapped, turning around and thrusting his face into Carrick's. 'I'd do nothin' underhand. And my deputy's business is his own — just happens to be in the same place that Fogarty was headed.'

Carrick shook his head: 'Sorry, Sam, just don't believe you.'

'Then go to hell and be damned,' Sam fired back, his voice low but his anger evident. 'You think I'm up to something — then you back it up.'

Leaning back, Carrick held his hands up as though fending off a suspected attack.

'Sam, I ain't saying nothing,' Carrick hastened to backpedal from a confrontation. 'I know you of old — and, true, I never seen you try a stunt like that. But I got to be wary. Like they say, there's a first time for everything.'

'Not much you could do anyways.' Sam relaxed and took a sip of his beer. 'After all, you said Stanton was out of your jurisdiction.'

'True,' Carrick agreed. 'But until some court comes to a decision Stanton's out of yours.'

'So there's no point to this argument?' Sam declared.

'Still need to know what your deputy's up to,' Carrick pushed, gently. 'Just so that I know. I mean, I watched that kid the other day, looking for all the world as though he was watching the girls go by. Didn't fool me none.'

'But?'

'He fooled Dawson.'

'Figured,' Sam nodded in agreement. 'A by-the-book man?'

'Rigid,' Carrick admitted. 'Nothing to stop him bringing Fogarty in. It's only the town that's in dispute — not the ranch.'

'Stanton's spread must be the biggest around here?' Sam probed by asking what appeared to be an innocent question.

'Once upon a time,' Carrick recalled. 'Take you two, maybe three days to get from one end to the other. That was 'til the damned Yankees carved it up. Trouble was that Arch Stanton died fighting the Reb cause and that's where the problem lay. Back taxes. Stanton's boy, Boyd, couldn't pay up but Porter Coleman could and grabbed the lion's share.'

'What happened to Stanton, then?' Sam took a thoughtful sip of his beer.

'Tried to hold on to what he'd got left,' Carrick answered. 'He didn't have a lot of stock and what he had was wiped out with tick fever. You see, Coleman brought up a bunch of longhorns out of Texas. They were riddled with the disease and just about threatened every ranch in spittin' distance. And don't forget it was all open range back in them days. Didn't make Coleman popular, anyways. Not sure what happened next — but

Coleman got shot of them longhorns at a hefty loss. Opinion is that he took them down Mexico way. Maybe sold them cheap for leather and tallow, but that ain't gospel.'

'Well, it's obvious that Coleman bounced back,' Sam observed.

'Yeah, Coleman's done well,' Carrick agreed. 'Unlike Stanton — he never recovered. When he went bust his wife and kid left him. But it all happened just before I came here. Stanton became reclusive and, mostly, farmed the land around the house. Vegetables, pigs, chickens and a small herd of dairy cows. Mostly to feed himself — but he had no forgiveness for Coleman. Several times Coleman tried to buy Stanton out but, like a stubborn fool, he just held out. Held out, that is until Matt Jaeger took over. That just adds to the mystery and we'll never know the answer to that one.'

'Why's that?' Sam asked.

'Well, not from Stanton,' Carrick replied. 'Boyd Stanton deposited his cash in the bank. Then booked a room in the Cattleman's Hotel — blew his brains out in Room 24.'

Carrick chuckled, which caused Sam some concern for he would have liked to have been let in on the joke.

'Room 24,' Carrick repeated between bouts of laughter. 'That was — that was the room that Coleman used when he stayed in town.'

Sam, too, began to laugh now that he was privy to the joke. So it was with good humour that he got up and went to the bar to get fresh beers for himself and Carrick. It was an opportunity to start thinking about what he had been told and piece in the threads of gossip that he had heard. Apart from background there was still nothing to start drawing the threads together. All he had was conjecture and possibilities. Maybe, he mused, another drink would loosen Carrick up some.

'So what happened to Stanton's wife?' Sam asked, as he returned to the table and slid the cool glass of beer to his companion.

Carrick shrugged: 'Went north. That's what the talk was, anyway. Like I say, I wasn't around at the time.'

'You said,' Sam said, a touch hazily. 'Forgot that.'

'Something I know for sure,' Carrick volunteered. 'When Coleman hit these parts he was no cowman. Hadn't a clue — not 'til Aldo Lund turned up to show him the ropes. Spent the best part of a year running Coleman's spread.'

'Aldo Lund?' Sam repeated, suddenly aware of a familiar name. Then he recalled that Dawson had mentioned that it was Aldo Lund who had bought out Stanton. Damned old age, he thought, be forgetting my own name next. So now it was easy for him to deduce that, after spending time with Coleman, Lund would have known all about Stanton's situation. But then he realized that he still had not uncovered the connection between Lund and Matt Jaeger. After all, it was Jaeger who was running Lund's spread.

'Aldo Lund,' Carrick repeated, surprised that the marshal had questioned the name. 'You should've remembered him. I do, from my Ranger days. He had a big spread just across the border down Mexico way. Things making a connection? It's what you're after, ain't it?'

Sam nodded with a grin, knowing that Tom Carrick had outfoxed him for once.

'And to finish the job,' Carrick said with a flourish, 'Elvira Lund married Matt Jaeger. Though I doubt if Lund was mixed up in any funny business. May have known what Jaeger was up to and, maybe, steered his son-in-law towards the right buyers. But the Aldo Lund we knew was straight and honest as you could get.'

Carrick took a long swig of beer, then set the glass back down on the table top. As he did so a shadowy figure caught his attention in the corner of his eye. He glanced up in time to see a figure in a black tailored suit and derby turn away and thread his way through the crowd.

'Damn it,' he cursed, as he half-rose from his chair.

'Problem?' Sam asked, with concern.

'Vance Traven,' Carrick answered, as though his companion should know who he was talking about. 'Traven said that if his brother hanged — then he'd come for me. Looks like he has.'

There was something in the sheriff's tone which suggested that Carrick was in two minds about going after Traven. Sam had never known the man to lose his nerve. But, all things considered, including the fact that Carrick was on his own, Sam saw no alternative but to stand by a friend.

'Need a hand?' Sam offered, as though it had to be done.

'Not your business,' Carrick warned, stiffly.

'I know Traven — he's fast,' Sam reminded him, adding: 'Never knew he had a brother, though.'

'You wouldn't think they were

140

brothers,' Carrick grimaced. 'Vance is the wild one while Jesse — well, Jesse worked hard down the livery. Got himself involved in a card game and was losing, heavily. Figured someone was cheating — you know the story. Anyway, seemed the dead man had a lot of friends and, well, it looks like the evidence went against Jesse.'

'And you don't think — ' Sam began, but Carrick held up his hand.

'I thought it was self-defence,' Carrick said, forcefully. 'But Traven's here — so, I guess Jesse was found guilty.'

For a few moments Tom Carrick stood there thoughtfully, chewing the inside of his mouth before deciding that it was time to deal with the situation.

'Right, Sam,' he nodded. 'Let's go get this thing done. And you're deputized — just to make it legal.'

'Obliged,' Sam grinned, standing up and buttoning his coat behind him so that his pistol butt would be free from obstruction.

Carrick shook his head: 'No — it's

me who should be thanking you. I just hoped that it would never have come to this.'

'That's life for you,' Sam murmured. They began to weave through the crowded saloon.

'One thing, though,' Carrick mentioned, bravely. 'Just what is your deputy up to? You never said and I'd hate to die without knowing.'

'That's always been your weakness,' Sam laughed. 'Curiosity. You always got to know.'

'It's that what's kept us alive this long,' Carrick pointed out.

Sam stopped dead in his tracks, his eyes fixed to the saloon's batwing doors, as he made a decision.

'My deputy has gone home,' he explained. 'Tom Ford was his pa.'

Carrick's jaw dropped: 'Tom Ford's boy? Chris? The one that beat seven bells out of his father? You have to be kiddin' me.'

'Hell's teeth,' Sam swore softly. 'I never knew that.'

'How long you known him?' Carrick asked, with instinctive disbelief. 'Tell you, when it happened the news spread like wildfire. There were folks here who couldn't believe that someone had taken Tom Ford down.'

'Didn't know he had family,' Sam admitted. 'Not 'til a couple of days ago.'

'And he's gone home?' Carrick queried with concern. 'Then he's ridin' into a hell of a mess. You know, I figure he might just need a friend.'

'Let's get this other mess sorted first,' Sam suggested. His words were meant to bolster the town marshal rather than allow his mind to worry about his deputy's predicament.

Letting out a deep sigh, Carrick nodded, then strode purposefully towards the batwings. He pushed them open and stepped out on to the boardwalk. All the time his eyes roved, trying to locate Traven, hoping to find him before Traven gunned him down in cold blood.

'Evenin', Marshal,' the flat voice

echoed across the suddenly empty street. 'Heard tell someone gunned you down.'

Carrick turned to glance over his shoulder at the man to whom the greeting had been addressed. 'Then just consider me a ghost,' Sam offered, watching the black-suited man detach himself from the shadows opposite and step down into the street.

'Figure you're buyin' inta this,' Traven deduced.

'Always stood by my friends,' Sam kept his tone light and friendly.

'We don't need to do this,' Carrick butted into the conversation.

' 'Fraid we do,' Traven answered. 'Made a promise — wouldn't do my rep any good if I broke it.'

Having said this Traven drew. He was fast but though he caught Carrick unawares, the lawman was able to get a shot in that made Traven stagger back. Even so, Traven raised his gun arm, but failed to trigger a second shot as Sam blasted two bullets into him. The bullets smashed into his chest, forcing him back and over the hitch rail opposite. Sam strode over and stared down at the hunched-up body, then holstered his weapon. He walked back to where Carrick was sitting on the steps outside the saloon. People began to flock towards the corpse like vultures anxious for the feed.

'He was fast,' Carrick gasped, white-faced and sweating.

'Fast — yes,' Sam nodded. 'But you put a bullet in him.'

'He got me too,' Carrick whispered.

Sam hunkered down beside him and saw that the town marshal's hand, gripping his side, was covered in blood.

Sam leaped to his feet, grabbed the first person to hand and sent the man off to fetch the doctor, with an angry promise of what he would do if the man failed to do it. Then he returned to his friend.

'Is this how it ends?' Carrick asked, coughing.

'Hell's teeth, Tom,' Sam snapped,

angry at the way things had turned out. 'I ain't died yet — so I don't know.'

'Well, I figure I'll have to come back.' Carrick laughed, which produced another coughing spell before he could say. 'I'll let you know.'

Sam laughed, too, but his mind was more on the time it was taking for the doctor to arrive on the scene. Also, he noticed that for a town that prided itself on keeping the streets safe for its citizens there was no sign of Dawson or a single deputy.

'Oh, hell,' Carrick grumbled, weakly. 'I think I've wet my pants.'

'Don't worry 'bout that,' Sam reassured him. 'You ain't in control of your functions. Happens.'

As he was speaking a thin, pale-faced man wearing a denim shirt and faded Levis squatted down by Carrick's side.

'OK, let's have a look,' he said.

'Who are you?' Sam demanded.

'The doctor,' the man replied, paying attention to his patient by pulling Carrick's hand away from the wound and opening his shirt. 'I do believe you sent for me.'

'Took your damned time,' Sam stated.

'Looked at the other feller first,' the doc told him as he examined the wound. 'Didn't fancy the idea of having him resurrect himself and shoot me.' He glanced up at Sam. 'Besides, leaving a corpse lying around makes the place look untidy. As for Tom here, he was lucky. From where I'm sitting it looks like a nice clean in-and-out wound with nothing vital being damaged.' Then he added with a wry smile, 'Well, perhaps his dignity.'

'Don't think I like your tone, mister,' Sam felt as though he had been pushed as far as he was prepared to go with the doc's attitude.

'Mister, when your life is a dull routine of delivering babies, treating measles, mumps, colds, coughs, and lancing boils,' the doctor explained, 'then you'll be entitled to be cynical. A bullet wound like this is a novelty.'

147

Pala-faced, Carrick glanced up: 'You been here four years, Al, and you're sayin' you never treated a bullet wound before?'

'Only idiots who shoot themselves in the foot,' came the terse reply. 'Now, let's get you into my surgery. Been dying to try out my butchery skills.'

Carrick held up his hand before Sam could make another comment.

'It's fine, Sam,' Carrick explained. 'It's a joke between us. Al Jennings here owns the butcher shop and he can do a fine . . .'

Al looked down at the prostrate lawman and said: 'He's just passed out, that's all.'

Between them they carried Carrick down the street and up the side stairs of the butcher's shop to where the doctor had his rooms. Carefully, they laid the lawman down on the examination table, where the doctor got to work.

'Don't go away,' Al suggested. 'He'll want a friend around when he wakes up.'

Sam just nodded as he slipped out of the room to sit in one of the two straight-backed chairs in the hallway that, no doubt, served as a waiting room. It was not long before the fatigue of the day caught up with him and he fell asleep. Though he slept his mind was filled with images, from the shoot-out at Dennett Junction to the recent events. By the time he woke, an hour later, he was still dwelling on the fragility of life.

Quickly he buried his thoughts and turned to the need to know how Tom Carrick was faring.

'Ah, you're awake,' the doctor observed as he peered around the door of the room opposite. Abruptly, Sam stood up and asked: 'How is he?'

'Bruised and dazed,' the doctor replied. 'What did you expect? To see him sitting in my parlour sipping a cup of tea as though nothing had happened?' Then he dropped the sarcasm. 'He's sleeping. The wound was clean and nothing important was damaged.

Right now he's healing and all I can do is re-dress the wound from time to time. The rest is down to his body and a certain will to live. If you want to see him then I suggest you come back in the morning.'

'I'll do that,' Sam conceded, knowing that there was nothing more that he could do. 'Got something to do first.'

'Let me guess,' Al said, with a broad smile. 'You want to give our courageous Dawson a going over. Save your energy and leave our Tom to sort out that problem. It's been a long time coming — but I think that our dear sheriff's days are numbered. It seems that you have a problem of your own to deal with — so Tom won't take it the wrong way if you choose to ride on.'

'I'll drop by before I go,' Sam promised. He turned towards the door, ready to let himself out.

'Up to you,' said the doctor. 'But before you go, Tom asked me to tell you this: Coleman, Ford and Jaeger — there was a time when they wore Yankee blue.'

Slowly, Sam turned around and for a moment he seemed to tower over the doctor: 'Why the hell didn't he tell me that before? Hell's teeth. How come he knew that?'

'I told him. I was their medical officer,' the doctor explained. 'Tom's my friend, too. So I know I can trust you with my little secrets. Remember, I know stuff about you — Tom often brings up anecdotes about you and him in the Rangers.'

Sam chuckled. 'When I come back this way I think I might drop by and share some tales with you.'

'You do that, Sam.' The doc grinned with a twinkle in his eye.

By the time Sam climbed into bed, back at the boarding house that had been home for the last couple of days, the evening's events had been put into perspective. As he recalled the conversation with the doctor he realized that there were questions that he should have asked. Still, he decided, tomorrow was another day.

9

Night fell on Stanton in a blazing sunset that reflected molten gold from the windows of the stores opposite the law office. Most of the stores were closed or in the process of closing down. Soon a stillness would settle over the town.

Down the street two riders came into town. Both rode easy without any sense of rush about them as they steered their mounts towards the hitch rail outside the law office. Every so often they would glance towards the general store, where a group of men was gathering. Although there was nothing unusual about this it was apparent that something had caught the riders' attention. The talk between them had become more animated in the last few minutes.

'Town Council,' Matt Jaeger's deep voice growled from inside the darkened law office. 'Seems like something's got their dander up.'

Perry Jaeger did not respond as he slid from the saddle and hitched his horse to the rails. Nor did his companion, a tall, rawboned man with a sour expression on his face who looked at the gathering with distaste. Pete Dwyer hated things going on that he knew nothing about. It just made him nervous.

'They's all goin' inside,' he observed, as he climbed the step on to the boardwalk. 'Ain't meetin' day. You figure they's up to somepin'?'

Although Matt Jaeger heard the question he chose not to air his thoughts on the matter until the other two men were inside the office.

'Sorry we're late,' Perry offered. 'Gramps proved a little difficult. And Ma would like it if you got home as quick as — '

'I'll be there presently,' Matt answered, his eyes still fixed on the general store — the doors of which were firmly shut. 'For now, Perry, I want you to keep an eye on things. Pete — you'll be coming back with me.' On seeing the quizzical look on Dwyer's face he added: 'Be grateful — I'm handing you a night off.'

'Problems?' Perry asked, anxious to find out what his father knew.

Matt Jaeger sat down behind the desk and looked around the small office as though searching for inspiration. It was not going to be easy to tell Perry what he had seen that day, and when he did he would need to handle it with care. He just hoped that Perry would not give in to temptation and do something stupid.

'Depends,' he answered. 'A stranger rode into town early this morning. Stopped by at the store opposite and came out empty handed. Then he went up the cemetery and — well, I guess from that that the missing Ford boy has arrived.'

'And that bothers us — why?' Perry wondered. He screwed up his face, unable to see the importance of this piece of information.

'Because while he's around,' Matt answered, 'we give him a wide berth.' He stood and picked up his hat. 'No one goes near Chris Ford — no one makes it their business to cause him to look in our direction.'

'Whatever you say, Pa,' Perry said. 'Only why should we? He ain't — '

'He ain't like his brothers,' Matt interrupted firmly. 'When he rode into town I knew I'd seen his face before. When I saw him go into the Ford house I figured him to be Tom Ford's missing boy.'

Matt Jaeger put on his hat, slipped his coat from the back of the chair and put it on. While doing this he came to the conclusion that he should come clean with his son.

'I figure the Ford boy could be Sam Ward's deputy,' Jaeger confessed.

The announcement was met with stunned silence. Both Perry and Dwyer stood there with expressions of blank astonishment on their faces. Despite the instinct to leave and go home, Jaeger stepped back into the office.

'Perry?' he prompted, peering closely at his son whose jaw was pulsating away as he kept his anger in check.

'Jus' coincidence,' Dwyer offered. 'Has to be. He'd not know Fogarty was here.'

Fogarty's name jerked Perry back into the present as he realized that it would be their connection with Fogarty that would bring the family to Ford's notice.

'You got to come to a decision, Pa,' Perry blurted out. 'We should get shot of Fogarty. I told you he was trouble.'

Matt nodded: 'Then I'll deal with it. Liam's my problem — not yours.'

Perry rounded on his father: 'Ain't just your problem. With Fogarty around everything you've done could be thrown away. Can't you see that?' He moved closer to his father who was staring fixedly at the floor. 'Me and Clint, neither of us would cross you, Pa, but we came close to it when we found out what Fogarty had done. If you're right, that deputy's right on our doorstep. There's nothing to think about. Nothing to deal with — except tell Fogarty to move on. Or let Billy take care of the problem.'

Jaeger's head jerked up on hearing what Perry's solution was. His immediate response was a surge of anger, and he fought it down. Part of him felt that it was time for Fogarty to move on. At the same time he wanted to stay loyal to a friend, after all no law could touch Fogarty as long as he did not come into Stanton.

It would have been easy to do nothing but there was something about Fogarty that made him uneasy. Maybe there would have been a chance to deal with Chris Ford if Fogarty had not left men behind to kill the marshal.

'This is how it works, Perry,' Jaeger explained, looking his son in the eyes. 'If I mess things up I'll walk away and leave you to deal with Fogarty. In return you give me twenty-four hours to come up with a solution.'

Perry thought about the offer for a while. It was a fair deal — not exactly satisfactory but it would have to do. The way he saw it was that his father would come through for the sake of the family.

One way or another.

'What about Ford?' Dwyer put in. 'You ain't forgettin' we's all wanted men where he comes from. He'd likely as not want to bag us all if'n he can.'

'I know that, Pete,' Jaeger acknowledged. 'Just as I know what's at stake here. But there's something that neither of you has considered.' He paused and looked at each man in turn, hoping that they could read his mind. When they remained silent he had no alternative but to remind them: 'He'll also be looking for the man who killed his pa. And if it was Billy and you know it, Pete, you'd best say so now.'

'Pa, you know — ' Perry exploded,

stepping in front of Dwyer as though to protect him.

Pete pushed him to one side and stepped up to face Jaeger. His face was set firm but he felt uncomfortable as he stood up to his boss.

'There was a shot, Mr Jaeger,' Dwyer said, keeping his voice level but forceful so that there was no doubt about what he was saying. 'The sheriff came into the saloon, but — but before he drew his gun Billy had drawn his. But it weren't him that done the shootin'. He may be stupid and want to prove hisself — but it weren't him who shot the sheriff. Ain't none of us would back him up if'n he'd done it.'

Jaeger nodded: 'That's what I figured from what Clint said. Let's hope Ford is man enough to accept that. Now, I'm going home.' As he reached the door he turned back to his son. 'And Perry, I counted seven men going into that store earlier — see how many come out. They're up to something and you know how I hate surprises.'

10

The evening meal in the Ford house had been a silent affair.

It was evident that Charlie had no liking for the fact that he had to sit at the same table as Chris. While Hal didn't really know what to do except pass whispered comments to his mother, who shushed him while letting the other two know that she was not happy with their behaviour at her table. She did this with the way she looked, mostly directed at Charlie, but a few glances were thrown Chris's way.

Even the way she noisily collected the plates and placed them in a bowl on the counter emphasized her discontent at her sons' rudeness.

'Well,' she said at last. 'If nothing else, having you three here means that I can deal with something that your pa wanted sorted out.'

'Not now, Ma,' Chris said firmly. He scraped his chair back and stood up. 'There is something I have to do.'

'Yeah, like get down the livery and leave,' Charlie invited, harshly. 'You've overstayed your welcome.'

Unexpectedly, Hannah shot across the room and delivered a stinging flat handed blow across the side of Charlie's face. Stunned, he half-leapt to his feet, ready to retaliate. Then he slumped down in shame at the thought that he could have acted violently towards his mother.

'Is it important?' Hannah asked, her watchful eyes on her eldest while the question was directed at Chris.

'To me, yes,' Chris acknowledged. 'Only be a few minutes — but it's got to be done.'

Hannah nodded: 'Thank you for telling me. What I had to say can wait a while.' Then she turned to Charlie. 'And, while Chris is gone, you can help me with the dishes.'

Chris collected his coat from the hall

stand and left the house by the kitchen door. Though eyebrows were raised at his actions, no one questioned his motives.

He stood at the back of the house for a while, just watching the last rays of the sun as it disappeared over the horizon. For a moment it looked like as though a prairie fire was raging in the distance, then it was gone.

As he strolled past the backs of the stores, some of which had vegetable patches like his ma's, he thought how easily his mother had given way. Maybe she just found it easier to give him his head than to do or say something that would drive him away again.

He knocked on Fred Harris's back door. It was answered by Harris's small, birdlike wife. She greeted him with a faint, welcoming smile and directed him to the parlour.

As soon as he entered the room fell silent. The seven men sitting around the table looked up at him but no one said a word. Instead they dropped their eyes as though recalling the day of the shooting.

'You all know why I'm here?' Chris asked, waiting to be invited to fill the vacant seat by Harris.

The only response was Harris's taking the badge from his vest pocket and sliding it across the table. Chris eyed it but made no move to take it.

'No objections?' Chris was a little surprised that not one of them could talk to him.

'Only me.' The speaker was soft-spoken and a stranger to Chris.

'We've covered the ground, Ryan,' Harris objected, glaring at the speaker. 'And took a vote. Six to one and the majority voted 'yes'.'

The man called Ryan was tall and slim, no more than thirty years old. His hair was oiled and slicked back. His beard, though thick, was neatly trimmed. In his dark-blue suit he looked more like a gambler but Chris figured him for a store clerk.

'I'm Ryan Eckersley,' he announced

importantly, as though advertising himself. 'I run the leather goods store.'

'Makes a fine saddle,' Uriah Bolton, the liveryman, chipped in. 'Real craftsman is Mr Eckersley.'

'I'm sure he does,' Chris acknowledged, his face deadpan, for he did not take to this man's attitude. 'More interested in why he objected.'

'Nothing personal.' Eckersley was quite expansive. 'And, God knows, I agree with everyone here that it's not good having Jaeger sitting in the sheriff's office and lording it about. But our previous sheriff — well, his reputation was suspect.'

'Don't beat about the bush, Ryan,' Chris suggested, drawing a little satisfaction from the way the man winced at the use of his given name. 'Pa was on the take. Getting backhanders from the Jaegers. Turning a blind eye to the rustling that was going on. And you think that having another Ford enforcing the law would be a mistake. Right or wrong?'

'Not quite,' Eckersley was definitely discomforted by the softly spoken but forceful words.

'Exactly quite,' Bolton mimicked the last word.

With a nod, Chris picked up the badge and put it in his pocket. As he took one last glance around the table he noticed that Ryan was glaring at him. His head was cocked at an angle with almost a challenging look about him while the middle finger of his right hand seemed to scratch at the hairs of his beard close to his chin.

It was only a minor thing, probably a habit, but that gesture jogged a memory that Chris couldn't place.

He dismissed the thought and decided it would be best to get out of the place.

'Well, gentlemen,' he said, 'at seven tomorrow morning I'll be in that office. Until then I'd be obliged if you kept this to yourselves.'

He turned to walk out of the room. Then, as though a thought had just occurred to him he turned back.

'Just one thing, Ryan,' he said. 'Where were you the night my pa was killed?'

Eckersley frowned, his middle finger once again scratching at his beard. 'In my store. I was fixing a saddle for Porter Coleman in my workshop — at the back. Why?'

Chris just shrugged: 'No reason. It's just that I know these other fellers were in the saloon. Don't remember your name being mentioned.'

'I don't drink.' Ryan offered as though it was an excuse.

'To each their own,' Chris grinned. Then he backed away and left the parlour. He had no reason to stay, for he had collected what he had come for. It was just a relief to be out of that store and away from people who resented him for what he had done.

'Seen Fliss?' Uriah Bolton, who had followed, called out to him.

Chris was tempted to ignore the question and walk on. He would have done if anyone else but the liveryman had asked that question.

'No,' he replied.

'You should,' the liveryman advised, but said nothing more before he stepped back into the store.

He hadn't deliberately forgotten about Fliss Lloyd. They had known each other at school and it had been a relationship that had blossomed. Sooner or later, or so folks thought, it was only a matter of time before they got hitched. But when he had walked away he had left her too. He'd not said a word to her; he had simply dismissed her from his mind.

Now, a simple question had reawakened his memories of happier times and he did not want that. Fliss belonged to the past and it was better that she stayed there. He hoped that they would manage to avoid each other — something that would suit him.

Fliss was still on his mind as he walked into the kitchen. Instantly, she faded away as it registered that his mother was sitting at the head of the table with a small, black tin box in front of her. On either side sat her other two sons. He wondered if they had sat here, waiting, all the time that he had been gone.

His mother gestured for him to take the seat at the opposite end of the table. Obediently, he followed the indicated request and sat with his back to the stove. Charlie glowered at him while Hal chose to stare at the grain on the table's surface. Hannah Ford opened the black box and removed three items, which she placed neatly in front of the box. Two packets wrapped in brown paper, one thick the other thin, that she placed either side of a large iron key. Chris recognized it as the key to his father's office. It drew an expectant glance from Charlie.

Hannah closed the box and put it to one side but not before she had placed a simple-looking document down in front of him.

'Boys,' she announced formally. 'This

is your pa's will. When he took on the job of this town's sheriff he thought it wise to go to Carfax and make sure that things were sorted out.'

She paused to straighten the pages.

'First, the house,' she began. 'The house stays with me until I die. After that it passes to you three boys. Your pa said that each of you should have a home to come home to.' She glanced at Charlie. 'That includes Chris — understand?'

'Doesn't mean I have to like it,' Charlie grumbled, but he caught the look in his mother's eyes and drew back from giving full vent to his feelings.

Hannah picked up the slim package and passed it to Hal.

'Hal, your father left you the workshop and the lumberyard,' she explained. 'He had all the deeds drawn up when he made his will.'

Next she picked up the key. For a moment she weighed it in her hand then scooted it down the table. Charlie went to grab it, but it was travelling too quickly and it finished up in Chris's lap.

Charlie held out his hand towards his brother: 'I'll take that, if you don't mind.'

'To Chris,' his mother went on, forcing Charlie to switch his attention back to her. He just stared at her with his mouth agape.

' 'To Chris,' ' Hannah continued, reading from the document now, ' 'I leave the contents of my office in the hope that he will discover something of me. Also in my office are ledgers relating to my business affairs. I would wish him to benefit from them.' '

Chris stared at the key as though he had been handed the keys to hell. He had no interest in his father's business and could only see the bequest as a pay-off for the guilt his father must have felt.

'Charlie,' Hannah placed the larger packet in front of her eldest son. 'In your lifetime you have had everything that a parent can give to a child. And you have taken it — but given nothing back. You have taken as though it were a right and not something that should be earned. Your father was tempted to leave you nothing but he changed his mind. In that package is two thousand dollars. It's your stake in life. Personally, I think you'll just fritter it away and have nothing to show for it. Your choice but I hope, for your sake, that you use it to make your own mark.'

Pale-faced, Charlie stared at the package. Then he stood up and backed away from the table. He was lost and unable to grasp what had just happened to him. Though he glanced at Hal and Chris they could offer no answers and any anger that he felt refused to rise. Unable to say anything he ran from the kitchen and did not stop until he got to the saloon.

Hannah said no more. She just closed the tin box, stood up and, leaving the other two sons alone, retired to the sitting-room.

'I don't understand.' Hal shook his head. 'Pa leaving everything to us two. I mean, shouldn't this be Charlie's?'

'Pa was always a law unto himself,' Chris responded softly, his concentration on the key that he turned over and over in his hands.

No one had ever seen the inside of Tom Ford's study. All their lives the children had been forbidden to enter this room. When their pa was not around the door was always locked and the key placed in their mother's care.

'He's still playing us up one against the other,' Hal remarked, breaking into his brother's thoughts.

'No, Hal,' Chris replied with a sigh. He scraped back his chair and stood up. 'He told us that, despite everything, he knew his children. That's why you've got the workshop, the tools and the yard. Because you'll use it all wisely and not run it into the ground.'

'Like Charlie would?' Hal questioned, looking up at his brother who stood by his side.

Chris nodded.

'But you run the business side,' Hal

continued, perplexed. 'That's what I figure from what Pa said.'

'You know more about that side of things,' Chris offered. 'I'm not going to interfere. Besides, I doubt if Pa intended me to run your business.'

'What do I do about that new saloon?' Hal suddenly thought. 'Charlie's been running things down there.'

'Hal, don't ask me.' Chris felt a little exasperated by Hal's indecision. 'It's your business — you deal with it.'

Hal said something in response but Chris ignored him. His brother's problems meant nothing to him. He walked up the hall and stood outside the door to the study. With mixed feelings he slid the key into the lock and twisted it but let his hand fall away from the handle.

Unlocking doors was one thing but going through them was another. He wondered if he really did want to know what his inheritance was. The will had talked of business interests but Chris only knew of one. What else could his father have been involved in?

The only way he could answer that question was by entering the room.

The room was dark, almost forbidding, for his father's presence was there. The smell of pipe tobacco, leather and wood lingered in the air — it was as though it was physical. Yet he had no desire to run. He picked up a flickering candle from the hall stand, entered and closed the door behind him.

In front of him was a mahogany bureau with its writing desk open. Above was a brass oil lamp which he lit before returning the candle to the hall.

Back at the bureau, he sat down in a straight-backed chair but still he did not feel comfortable about being there. Slowly, he looked around him taking in the stove flanked by bookcases against the far wall. Curious, he got up and had a look at the books, ran his fingers along the titles. A complete set of Fenimore Cooper's books captured his attention. Some were newer than others but it was *The Spy* that he chose to look at — the inscription inside was addressed to his grandfather, Robert. But when he took down *The Deerslayer* he was shocked to find that it was a gift to his father.

'He read them all, you know.'

His mother's voice made him jump, for he had not heard her enter.

'Your father said that you'd go straight to the books,' she continued, sitting down by the bureau. 'He used to read to you boys — well, Charlie and you. Even when you were a baby he guessed that you would be the reader in this family.'

'So what changed?' Chris dismissed what he felt was a clumsy attempt to reminisce about pleasant things.

'I don't know,' his mother confessed. 'He changed when his father died. You were about eight when that happened. He took Charlie out of school and decided that he would have to learn a trade but you he left to finish your schooling.

'You see, your father was an only

child. His father was — he was well off. He invested in property and in the slave trade. Your father had an expensive education and was expected to follow in his father's footsteps. But your father fell in love with wood and what could be done with it. There was quite an argument. In the end your grandfather gave your father five hundred dollars and sent him away.

'Of course, your father bought himself an apprenticeship and became his own man. By then, I had met him and he was doing well for himself. We married and had Charlie, you and Hal. Then the Civil War came.

'Your grandfather, sensing what the outcome would be, had transferred his funds to the north and moved to Maine. He put his money into munitions and made a profit. Even offered your father a job. But you know your father — he was a stubborn man and refused. Instead, he joined the army and when the war was over we came out here. Shortly after that his father died. That and his experiences in the war just changed him. I could make excuses for him — he so wanted you to be your own person.'

'Thanks for the history lesson,' Chris stated, bitterly. 'But that doesn't put things right. Telling me that and showing me this,' he waved his arm at the books, 'it makes no sense to me. So Pa had a tough time — that wasn't my fault. There was no need to take it out on me.'

Hannah shook her head: 'He made a mistake. He knew that he was taking his anger out on the wrong son.'

'Was that before or after I hit him?' Chris snorted, his eyes dark with anger.

'I think — ' his mother began, her tone indicating a defence was coming.

'Does it matter now?' Chris demanded. 'I would have preferred to have heard it from him, but he's conveniently died.'

'Then why did you come home?' Hannah demanded, rising to her feet ready to confront him.

'Because you asked me to.' He frowned.

'I didn't ask you,' Hannah pointed out. 'I just told you that your father had been killed. I thought that you needed to know that.'

'But I had to make sure that you were all right,' Chris protested.

'Why shouldn't I be all right?' his mother asked, scathingly. 'Charlie was here and so was Hal. So, just why did you come back?'

Tears began to well up in his eyes. They trickled slowly down his cheeks and on to his chin.

'I don't want to be here,' he sobbed into his mother's shoulder as she reached around to hold him tight. 'I don't want his books — or his business. I don't regret what I did — but I can't live with it any more. If — if I'd not gone away, maybe he would still be alive.'

'No, Chris,' she soothed. 'Your father always believed that the day a person died was already marked out. No one could have stopped it from happening.'

Chris had reached breaking point and, together, mother and son talked until the early hours of the morning. Some issues were resolved while others were left to him to decide what the next move was to be. Most of all he learned more about his father than he had ever known. His mother made no excuses but gave her son enough to make him understand.

Exhausted, his mother retired to bed while Chris began to go through the books. There were a lot of entries relating to the carpentry and building business. Surprisingly, there were rents being collected on four stores, one of which was the leather goods store owned by Ryan Eckersley. It turned out that when his father had moved to Stanton there had been five lots that were vacant. Tom Ford had bought them all but had chosen the best upon which to build his house.

The third ledger made him sit back. It had been clear from the first lot of accounts that Tom Ford had made enough money to get by on. Though there had been times when he had barely broken even. He could, therefore, understand his father taking up the badge, for it was a guaranteed forty dollars a month, which made a difference.

The third ledger made it quite clear that Tom Ford didn't need the money. This ledger contained the business accounts for Porter Coleman's ranch. From this Chris discovered that Tom Ford was getting a forty per cent share of the profits. Even as he was asking himself the question why he noticed that there was something at the back of the ledger. He flipped the pages over and found a document at the back. It was a partnership agreement. Quickly, he read it through. Although it didn't answer all his questions, he gained an insight, found a possible motive for his father's death. Maybe Coleman had wanted to terminate the partnership and had thought of an easy way to do it.

Just one problem, Chris mused. His father had been pretty clever in putting in that bit that covered his heirs. If Porter Coleman thought he was in the clear he had another think coming — for he had a new partner.

11

Chris was woken by the early-morning sounds of his mother preparing breakfast. He stretched and silently cursed himself for falling asleep sprawled across the bureau. Going through his father's papers had given an insight into the man that had been both interesting and frustrating at the same time. For although some questions answered themselves there were others that were not so clear-cut.

Quickly, he doused the lamp, left the room and slipped upstairs to the bedroom, where Charlie, still fully dressed, was sprawled face down on Chris's bed. Hal was in the process of getting dressed.

'Could do with some clean clothes,' Chris whispered.

'Got a shirt,' Hal pointed at the dresser. 'It's the red one. Ma bought it

but it's not for me. If you want pants
— I can't help you. I think I might be a
bit bigger than you.'

Chris grinned as he pulled open the
drawer and looked at the shirt. It was
bright but it would do for the time
being.

'I see what you mean,' he commented
as, out of curiosity, he opened the
middle drawer to find a pair of black
denim pants.

He pulled them out and wondered if
they would still fit. Only one way to
find out. They were snug and it pleased
him to know that, although he had
filled out in the last five years, he could
still wear his old clothes.

Together Hal and Chris went down-
stairs where Chris handed the study key
to his mother, who acknowledged the
gesture with a genuine smile.

'Still don't know what to do about
Charlie,' Hal confessed over breakfast.

'You let him know who's boss,' Chris
told him. 'Tell him he still has a job
— if he wants it.'

'Easy for you to say,' Hal replied. 'Charlie's not a doer — he likes to dish out the orders. As it's your business now, wouldn't it be easier if you told him?'

'You do it,' Chris suggested, pointing his knife, in emphasis, at his younger brother. 'Prove to me that you can handle the situation and get the job done. Do that and we'll talk some more about whose business it is.'

Hal gaped at him while their mother looked on with a touch of admiration in her eyes. For it seemed to her that there was a change in the bitter, angry young man who had just returned home.

'Well, I'd better get out there and do that,' Hal seemed a lot more cheerful as he finished his breakfast and stood up.

When he had gone, Hannah came over and took his place.

'That was a kind gesture,' she smiled.

'Face it, Ma, it's not kindness,' Chris said. 'He knows the business and I don't. It should be in his hands.' Without giving her the opportunity to make a remark he continued: 'So what's the deal with Porter Coleman?'

'Nothing much,' his mother told him. 'They were in the army together. When your father came West Porter came along too. They were quite close back then. Porter was looking to become a cattleman and when a parcel of land came up — well, your pa gave him a helping hand. He could've made it a loan but they did a deal, with your pa being a silent partner. Porter made a hash of things to start off with — lost his herd. So Pa stepped in again and stumped up the cash for a new herd. That's when he had a proper agreement drawn up.'

'So, why the enmity now?' Chris pressed. 'I mean, I hear that Coleman's accusing Pa of having taken bribes.'

Hannah shook her head: 'I really don't know. Perhaps, you should ask Porter.'

'Perhaps I will.' Chris nodded thoughtfully.

'Be careful,' Hannah pleaded. 'You

won't have the law backing you up.'

Chris just grinned as he slipped the star from his vest pocket and pinned it to his chest.

'As of now,' he announced, 'I am the law.'

He gave her a moment to admire the badge.

'Just one thing,' he mentioned in passing, as he put on his coat. 'How come none of us boys ever heard of Pa being friends with Porter Coleman?'

His mother just smiled as though at a fond memory: 'Your pa was like that. Family, friends and business — they all had their place.'

Yeah, Chris thought. Just as he believed that he was beginning to understand his father, so more secrets began to emerge. He wondered just what would come up next.

He mulled over his thoughts as he strolled down the main street. It would be another hour or so before the stores started to open up. This suited Chris fine, for it meant that he could face

Matt Jaeger alone. There was, he considered, no need for the whole town to know their business. Jaeger was sitting behind the desk with his feet up and showed no intention of moving. However, he did look at his visitor with expectation.

'Been a long time, Matt,' Chris remarked. He took the opposite seat and spun it round, to sit astride it with his arms resting on the back.

'Figured it was you, Deputy.' Matt grinned, but his watchful eyes remained expressionless. 'Bit of a shock to find out you were Tom Ford's son.'

'That's life,' Chris acknowledged with a slight shrug.

'I'm sorry for your loss,' Matt sounded genuine. 'But you can't pin anything on me or mine.'

'That's what I hear,' came the even reply.

'I take it you're here for me anyway,' Matt assumed, with a sigh. 'Trouble is you're way out of your jurisdiction.'

Chris shook his head: 'Not here for

you. As for jurisdiction — I think you'll find that I have more right to be here than you do.'

'In what way?' There was a slight hint of challenge in Matt's uneasy tone.

Chris just let his coat hang open a bit more so that Jaeger could see the badge.

Matt laughed and slapped his thigh, then shifted his feet off the desk top: 'It figures. Should've guessed the moment you walked in here.' He pointed out of the window. 'Saw that bunch gathering at the store yesterday. Couldn't work it out. Seven went in and seven came out.'

'I came and went the back way,' Chris explained. 'Couldn't have you knowing all my business.'

'Well, you're here now,' Matt conceded, as he began to stand up, but Chris just gestured for him to remain where he was.

'I hate having proprietorial rights,' Chris explained, lightly. 'I don't care if you sit there but I do think we should have a little chinwag — don't you?'

Matt regarded the man opposite with suspicion. He was not sure which direction the conversation would take and it made him uneasy.

'Shoot.' Jaeger made the invitation plain.

'Just interested to know if the rumour was true,' Chris said. 'You know, the one about you paying Pa to look the other way.'

'No truth in it,' Jaeger snapped. 'All I know is that Coleman spread that word around. If that was my style there'd be a few lawmen doing nicely out of it — and you, *you*, Mr Ford, would've heard about it.'

'Have to admit that I agree with you,' Chris concurred, thoughtfully. 'But, as they say, first time for everything. Like you being here. I mean of all the places you could've hid out — you choose Stanton.'

Matt Jaeger sat quiet and thoughtful for a moment. He just stared out of the window as he debated about what he could say to the new sheriff before deciding that the truth would be the best way.

'To start a new life,' Matt said, simply. 'Put the past behind us. No doubt you heard that I got accused of rustling Coleman's cattle. There was no truth in it. As for the reason we came here — well, my father-in-law was ramrod for Coleman's outfit for a while. Got on quite well with Boyd Stanton as well. Tried to do him a favour and get his ranch going again. Stanton had had enough and had no time for Coleman, either. Don't ask me why, and Aldo never found out — but Aldo did come back with a promise from Stanton.'

'This is Aldo Lund we're talking about?' Chris pressed.

Matt Jaeger nodded, surprised that Chris knew the name.

'A very talkative lawman told me about Aldo,' Chris told him, taking no joy in the revelation. 'I'm going to have to come out and have a chat with him.'

Jaeger shook his head, sorrowfully:

'Can't do that. Any more than I can. Three years back he got trampled in a stampede — he's paralysed from the neck down. Can't speak — and I've no idea if he can hear, let alone see. We spend the time of day with him so that he knows what's going on. He sits out on the porch and we keep some of the herd close, just in case he can see. He was the reason we sold up — cut our herd by half and came up here. We all thought that we'd be coming to a place where no one would know us. Though, it nearly didn't happen.'

'Why was that?'

'Coming up to seal the deal.' Matt laughed. 'When you and that damned marshall got on my trail.'

'You're kidding,' Chris couldn't help but join in the laughter.

'No, that's the truth.' Matt grinned, then became serious. 'You know, just talking to you, I can see your pa in you. We got along fine — hope we can do the same.'

Chris stared at the other man in

disbelief. Hitherto had anyone mentioned how like his father he was he would have shot them down with a denial. Now, he sat before a man whom he had tried to bring to justice, only to find a man who spoke plainly and simply. He found himself liking the man for himself.

'And I'm damned sorry for your loss,' Matt said.

'Obliged.' Chris's response was slightly muted. Then recalled something that he had to do: 'Liam Fogarty with you?'

Jaeger nodded.

'I'll have to bring him in,' Chris stated, in a tone that suggested that there'd be no argument in the matter. 'He killed a man — and I know it.'

Slowly, Jaeger nodded in agreement. He was being handed a way out of an awkward situation and knew that he'd be a fool not to take it.

'I'll do you a deal,' he offered. 'I'll bring him in to town in the morning — as far as the livery. But I won't turn him over to you.'

'Fair enough,' Chris agreed, though curious. 'But why?'

'A show of good faith,' Jaeger stated. 'Anything else and I guess he'd run. Maybe go back to his old ways — and I wouldn't want anything to jeopardize what I've got.'

'Deal,' Chris offered his hand, which Jaeger took. 'But if you're not here by noon I'll come looking.'

'I know you will,' Jaeger acknowledged.

'One other thing,' Chris warned him. 'Ben Buell, Pete Dwyer, Billy McDonald and your boy, Clint — they're posted out of town until Pa's killer is caught.'

'Fair enough,' Jaeger agreed. 'Rather expected that. What about Coleman's men?'

'Same'll go for them,' Chris promised. 'I intend going to see Coleman myself and giving him the good news.'

Matt chuckled: 'Then luck to you. The way I hear it no one gets to see

Coleman unless he chooses to come to you.'

Chris pursed his lips for a moment, then said simply, 'Like I said before — first time for everything.'

Matt Jaeger stood up and stretched: 'Well, if you're done — I'd better be going.' He looked around him and shuddered: 'Be good to get away from this place. Gives me the creeps.'

'Bet it does,' Chris said, lightly. 'Nearest you've been to a cell, I reckon.'

'Too close.' Jaeger smiled, the lines around his eyes creasing up. 'I'll see you — tomorrow.'

Jaeger held out his hand in a friendly gesture that Chris could not ignore.

In his time Chris had learned that there were bad men and there were downright evil men. But when you got down to it there were those who, but for fate, would be well-meaning people. He could not help but feel that Matt Jaeger fell into that category.

They shook hands, then Chris watched the man leave the office, mount his horse and ride out of town. Suddenly, he had that feeling that he was being watched. Quickly he scanned the street, but there was no one to be seen. Gut instinct told him that trouble was coming and that it was not that far away.

Someone knew who his father's killer was — and that someone was right here in this town.

He made a quick tour of the street, stopping by at the building site but keeping his distance. No one was loafing today for Hal seemed to have taken charge and the workers were busy. He crossed the road, went past the livery, then the blacksmith's shop where Uriah's brother, George, was opening up. The blacksmith gave him a quick wave, which Chris acknowledged, before turning back to his chores. It was the only greeting he got until he reached the general store, but before that he had noticed the new eating-house, from which came the tantalizing smell of baking bread.

'Sorry about last night,' Fred Harris's apologetic voice brought Chris back to earth. 'There'd been a heated debate before you turned up.'

'Ryan Eckersley?' Chris questioned, though he knew the answer.

'Partly,' Harris admitted. 'Morgan — the barber — he wasn't so much against. Well, he's old-fashioned and goes on about morality and — '

'He dragged up the past,' Chris supplied for him, to save embarrassment.

'Exactly.' Harris sighed with relief. 'Left the air a bit sour. Just wanted to apologize.'

'It's fine,' Chris tried to reassure the storekeeper. 'I bet that Eckersley feller enjoyed that.'

'He's strange, that one,' Harris said, hastily, glad that the subject had changed. 'Keeps himself to himself most of the time. But he's one hell of a craftsman when it comes to working with leather.'

'Been around long?'

Harris looked around as though frightened of being overheard: 'Just over a year or so. Just behaves so oddly. I mean, take this for example — once a week I find a list of groceries that he needs. Sure, I take it round and he pays up — got no complaints there — but he rarely comes out of that store. We have a council meeting and he's there and takes an active role.' Harris screwed up his face and shrugged his shoulders. 'That's all anyone gets to see of him.'

'So — how'd he get elected?' Chris was curious to know.

'My fault,' Harris confessed. 'Took him his groceries one day. Mentioned that the doc had called time and that we had a vacancy. He just jumped in and put himself forward. No one else did — so there he was, right in.'

'Odd,' Chris mused.

'Very,' Harris agreed.

As they parted Chris noticed that the saloon was open, so he slid through the batwing doors into the dim interior, where Katy Lloyd, who preferred to be known by the initial 'K', was cleaning the tables.

'No Joe?' he commented.

Katy was a big-boned woman and tall, with a mass of black curly hair that rolled down to the middle of her back. She had a preference for black clothing and today she wore an off-the-shoulder blouse and pants.

She stopped what she was doing and came over to him. Wrapping her arms around him, she pecked his cheek before standing back to admire him.

'You're lookin' good, Chris,' she greeted him enthusiastically, before answering the question. 'No, Joe's skedaddled to Carfax. Got himself a job there that'll keep him busy there for the next few weeks. At least, he's out from under my feet.'

'No other reason?' Chris couldn't help but ask. Instantly he regretted it.

Katy threw him a steely look.

'Joe was behind the bar,' she said firmly, pointing to the far end of the bar, which ran the length of the saloon.

'Right up there when your pa was killed. They may have had a fallin' out in the past — but, you know Joe, he'd not be one to hold a grudge.'

'I know that.' Chris felt a little abashed that he had messed up what should have been a happy reunion. 'Joe hinted at what happened. But I want to find Pa's killer and I — '

'Chris!' The sharpness in her tone stopped him dead. 'I know all that and I s'pose you have to check everything. So I'll tell you — the killer was not in my saloon. He was gunned down from out there — from the street. You should go and talk to Porter Coleman. One of his men, Rufus Coverdale, was the last out. I heard the others light out while Coverdale was dawdling through those doors. It wasn't that long after your pa was shot.'

Chris knew that he was messing things up with his need to get as much information as possible. Even though he was getting what he wanted, he had managed to get on Katy's bad side in the process.

'Sorry, K,' he blurted out. 'I've handled this all wrong.'

'Don't be.' Katy shrugged with a slight smile. 'Friendships and jobs don't mix. You gotta ask, otherwise you don't know.' Then, swiftly, taking Chris off guard, she changed the subject. 'Seen Fliss yet?'

Ready to make a retort, Chris opened his mouth, then closed it. For this was a subject that he had to handle with care. It had been Katy who, ten years ago, had taken in the thirteen-year-old orphan, Felicity who, weak and hungry, had been found wandering by Boyd Stanton's boy out in the country. Although a search party had scoured the area, they found no sign of her parents or of where she could have come from. Even when she was stronger she had no recollection of the past few years. Those that she did have were those of a child who had played with dolls in a room that was the only place that she could describe. Nor was she aware of her own name, except that she was called Fliss.

With a young girl needing a name Katy had brought her up as her own — always in the hope that one day Fliss would remember something so that she could be reunited with her family.

'Not yet,' Chris admitted, carefully. 'I guess we have some things that need to be sorted out.'

'Well, just don't go raisin' your hopes,' Katy warned him with a satisfied look. 'She's got some traits offa me and I wouldn't want to be in your shoes when you two collide.'

'Doubt if I want to be, either.' Chris had to agree with her. 'If I can, I want to get this other thing seen to before I have to deal with Fliss.'

Katy laid a hand on his shoulder, a friendly gesture that was meant to calm him.

'Life's not built that way, Chris,' she told him, softly. 'You can't put things into boxes and open them when you need to. I know you'll be wantin' that killer, but I know Fliss, and sooner or later, if you don't go to her — then she'll sure as hell will hunt you down.'

Chris stepped away and walked to the saloon doors. Resting his arms along the top of the batwings he stared out into the street. He knew that Katy was right; there never would be a right time — not to face Fliss and deal with the issues that stood between them.

'Right,' he decided. 'I'll see her tonight. That's a promise.' He turned back to Katy: 'I take it she still lives here?'

Katy shook her head: 'She lives above the eating-house — the one next to Harris's store, in case you didn't notice.'

'What happened?' Chris wondered. 'I mean, why's she living there?'

'She owns the place,' Katy stated, as though he was stupid for not knowing that. 'Didn't your ma tell you?'

'No,' he said, biting his tongue. 'That's one thing she didn't tell me. I'm beginning to wonder what else she forgot to mention.'

There were a lot of things swimming around in Chris Ford's head as he crossed the road to the sanctuary of his office. A lot of it did not make any sense. The first thing that struck him was that when he left Carfax he had been dead certain that he was riding into a range war. Only there seemed to be no sign of one.

Matt Jaeger had set himself up as the law and, in doing so, had posted Porter Coleman and his crew out of town. For some reason that Chris couldn't fathom Coleman had simply rolled over and complied.

Secondly, there was the fact that his father been a silent partner in Coleman's ranch. Yet his father had kept those dealings separate from family life. The only reason that Chris could see for Coleman killing his father was to rescind the partnership. That was assuming that Coleman had wanted to buy Tom Ford out and Tom had said no. If Coleman had had anything to do with Tom Ford's death, then there must have been another reason. For Coleman, surely, would have known that even if he killed the sheriff there would be another Ford to take his place.

Third was that, the way he heard things, his father had been trying to keep the peace between the Coleman and the Jaeger crews. Knowing his father's temperament it would have made more sense to have backed up his partner.

Then something struck him. A well-meant sentence from a conversation when Matt Jaeger had hinted that he could see his father in him. It raised another question in Chris's mind. No man could make that kind of comment unless he knew his father.

12

Chris was reluctant to leave the office unattended but when he considered that the cells were empty and that this town was not like others he felt that he could leave and not worry about a thing. It was not as if there was anything worth stealing, except for his father's Henry rifle sitting in the rack next to the key peg by the entrance to the cell block.

The ring of keys he did remove and attached them to his gunbelt. He didn't want to come back and find that some well-meaning citizen had locked the door on him.

As he was locking the desk drawers, Charlie came charging in and flung himself into the chair.

'Just what is it with you lot?' he demanded, scowling at the floor with an intensity that suggested he hoped that he would find the answer there. 'I mean, what have I done, that Pa should do this to me? I've always been there for him. Never asked for anything. And I end up with the — '

'Shut up, Charlie,' Chris told him firmly. 'You come barging in here like a pregnant cow with its arse on fire and expect me to jump and put it out. You've made it plain that you want to see the back of me. Yet here you are, demanding that I sort your problems out for you.'

'Come on, Chris,' Charlie pleaded. 'We're brothers. We shouldn't be at loggerheads.'

'Right.' Chris nodded, his tone cynical. 'So, now we're brothers. Why don't you just come straight to the point and tell me what you want?'

Once again, and because he was not getting what he wanted, Charlie scowled at the floor.

'Hal told me I wasn't in charge.' His voice was petulant and spoilt. 'Said if I wanted to work there then he was fine with that. But Pa put me in charge.'

'That was when he was alive,' Chris explained, slowly and calmly. 'Things have changed. Hal's in charge — and that's because I own the business. I don't want someone down there who's going to strut around giving orders and not put their back into the work.'

'I put the work in,' Charlie protested indignantly, thrusting a threatening finger in Chris's direction.

'When I rode into town yesterday,' Chris pointed out, 'the men were sitting around doing nothing. Where were you? Up at the cemetery telling me to get out of town.'

'No, that's not right,' Charlie protested, rising angrily to his feet. 'I was there. I saw you ride into town. Saw you go straight up to the cemetery. I ran up after you.'

Chris, rather than anger his brother by calling him a liar, held up his hands: 'I'm not going to argue with you. I made my choice and I'm sticking with it. As for what you've done to deserve this, I suggest you think long and hard about that. Because you and me ain't done yet — but when I'm done finding Pa's killer, I'll be looking to settle accounts.'

The bitterness in Chris's tone was lost on his brother, who dismissed the warning as a threat, rather than the intended promise.

'You can't touch me,' Charlie spat as he got to his feet and headed for the door. 'Ma'll send you packing if you ever lay a hand on me. She didn't like it that you got what should've been mine. So you just make the most of what you got — 'cos soon it's going to be mine.'

'Is that why you killed Pa?' Chris asked softly, stopping his brother dead in his tracks.

Red-faced and looking ready to charge down on his brother, Charlie roared: 'I ain't like you. I'd never do anything to hurt Pa.'

For a long, tense moment the brothers locked stares, until Chris nodded and looked away.

'Just had to be sure, Charlie,' he said, calmly, almost wishing that his brother had done what he had just accused him of doing.

'Yeah, I bet,' Charlie growled as he left the office.

Charlie glanced back once before stomping up the street. No doubt he was going to whisper more poison into his mother's ear. And if last night's quiet conversation between her and Chris was anything to go by, she was bound to deliver all the right words that would continue to make Charlie believe that she was on his side. That had been his parents' fault for as long as he could remember. Charlie would gripe and they, tired of hearing the same old thing, would just grunt and Charlie would take it that they agreed with him. Seemed like nothing had changed.

In the office Chris sat down and allowed the tension to drain away. He could not go and see Porter Coleman while he was in this state. At least he had got one thing straight about

Charlie, and that was that his brother was not a killer. Had it been otherwise Chris would have struck out. He had no doubts about that — but then, Charlie had always been all mouth. The only time that Chris could recall when Charlie had gone into action was when he had had some cronies with him. Not that he had needed backup, for his victim had been seven years younger than he was. A small, timid eight-year-old who had accidentally bumped into him.

'Damn hell,' Chris growled into the empty room as he thumped a fist on to the desktop. 'That damn fool of a brother — '

Silencing himself before he said something that he would regret he stormed out of the office, slamming the door behind him. Once on the board-walk caution took over as he checked in all directions, for he could not trust his brother to have gone home. There was always the chance that he could have lingered, hoping for that chance to take

Chris unawares.

Fortunately there was no sign of Charlie. Chris felt a lot easier as he crossed the road and walked down to the livery.

No one was about, so he went to the stall and began saddling his horse. He was just tightening the cinch when a low cough announced that he wasn't alone.

'Goin' someplace?' Uriah Bolton asked, leaning both arms on the stall as he peered over to watch Chris at work.

'Got to see Coleman,' Chris answered, with a half-glance over his shoulder.

'They say Coleman don't see people,' Uriah pointed out. 'He wants to see you, he'll come in to town.'

'Heard that,' Chris nodded sagely. 'Like I told the other feller — first time for everything.'

'That's as maybe,' the liveryman sighed. 'But that badge don't have no authority beyond the town limits.'

'You're right,' Chris nodded, unpinned

the badge and slipped it into his vest pocket. 'I don't need to hide behind it. But one thing I do know. Coleman and I are going to have words.'

Uriah Bolton thumped the woodwork and burst out with a round of raucous laughter.

'Chris, I gotta hand it to you,' he bellowed. 'You're as stubborn a cuss as your pa.'

Chris led the horse out of the stall, his eyes twinkling as he glanced at the thickset, bald-headed and walrus-moustached liveryman.

'Maybe, Uriah, maybe,' Chris grinned easily.

'Seen Fliss yet?' Uriah asked, abruptly changing the subject.

Chris shook his head: 'Some things are best left as they are.'

'Oh!' There was something about the tone of voice that should have warned Chris.

Instead he did a complete turn and he staggered backwards until he collided with his horse. His face was burning all down the left side as though someone had thrown boiling water at him.

'Well, Christopher Ford, I don't think so,' roared a female voice that forced him to face his attacker.

She stood there, her red, angry face hidden by strands of her long black hair. Her eyes, what he could see of them, burned with emerald fire.

'You and me,' she continued, without a pause, thrusting her face into his, 'we got some talking to do. Tonight. My place. I'll let your ma know she don't need to set a place for you.'

Having had her say, she marched out of the livery, leaving two very stunned men in her wake.

'Was that Fliss?' Chris asked, rubbing the side of his face.

'Yeah,' Uriah said, finding it difficult to gape and talk at the same time.

'I think she might be a little mad at me.' Chris climbed ruefully into the saddle.

'Just be grateful you got slapped,'

Uriah told him. 'The last feller that upset her got laid out. Take my advice — you don't turn up — she'll come and find you. And it won't be pretty. Just glad I ain't in your shoes.'

'Well,' Chris chuckled, trying to laugh the incident off. 'At least she got it out of her system.' Uriah watched as Chris rode off but could not help addressing his back: 'Just don't believe it. She ain't done with you.'

★   ★   ★

The cool breeze on his face seemed to take some of the pain away.

Chris thought back to the kind, gentle girl with laughter in her eyes. Then he shut the vision away as he did not want to remember. But, like an itch he couldn't scratch, she resurfaced at the forefront of his mind. He had always known what folks had thought but he had never seen himself and Fliss as anything but friends. If she had seen things differently then that was her fault. He shouldn't — he wouldn't take the blame for that.

Without realizing it, because he was still thinking about what he'd say to Fliss, he had ridden past the old Stanton ranch and could see the wire fence stretching out in the distance. For a moment he thought about turning around. Coleman could wait another day. It would be better to sort out the problem with Fliss first, so that he would have an uncluttered mind when he faced the rancher.

The hell with it, he decided. Another hour or so and he'd be at the ranch. He had got this far, so he might just as well go on.

The sun had passed its zenith and was starting to create shadows again when Chris reined in at the entrance to Coleman's ranch. There he was met by a man on foot who held a rifle across his chest. Just away to his left was another on horseback. He too was armed, the rifle held in his right hand with the barrel slanting across his shoulder.

'Goin' someplace?' the man on foot asked.

Chris looked him over. Though the man was well built, there was youth in his face, and a fleshiness about his figure.

'Going to see Porter Coleman,' Chris informed him, politely.

'What makes you think Mr Coleman would want to see you?' the man asked, as the horseman edged closer.

'Name's Chris Ford.'

'Don't care what your name is.'

'Related to Tom Ford?' the horseman asked, keeping his distance but trying to give Chris the once over.

'His son,' Chris replied. 'I'm the new sheriff of Stanton.'

'Don't care who you are,' the man on foot told him. 'No one gets to see Porter Coleman. If he's got anything to say to you — he'll come to you.'

Deliberately, Chris slid from his horse making sure that it remained between him and the horseman.

'You know how many times I've been told that?' he asked the man in front of him. 'And yet here I am and — '

The man, concentrating on what Chris was saying didn't realize his intention until too late. Chris had held the waddy's eyes as he took a pace forward. Suddenly, without warning, he lunged forward and snatched the rifle from the man's hands. With a quick, upward jerk he slammed the butt into his jaw and sent him sprawling.

'Now, you,' he pointed the rifle at the horseman. 'Get rid of your weapons.'

Without taking his eyes off the horseman Chris stooped down and removed the semi-conscious cowhand's handgun. Satisfied that his orders had been obeyed he stood up but still kept the rifle trained on the horseman.

'Got a name?' Chris asked.

'Stan — Stan Hardiman,' the horseman croaked, not sure about what was going to happen next.

'Well, Stan, how about you escorting me to Porter Coleman?' Chris asked, remounting his horse.

'Mister, you don't know what you just done.' There was a quaver in Stan's tone. 'You just got me and Brad there fired.'

'We'll see about that,' Chris said curtly. 'Just take me to Coleman.'

'Do I have a choice?' Stan grumbled, staring down at Brad who had decided that it was better to play possum.

'Yes.' Chris grinned, though his eyes were cold.

'I do?' Stan sounded surprised.

Chris nodded as he pointed up the rutted track. 'Just lead the way.'

Chris followed Stan for a mile up the track to the top of a knoll. Then down towards a two-storey, white-painted, board house. As they approached four men suddenly came out of the adjoining barn. They positioned themselves across the front of the house.

'Coleman seems to need a lot of protection,' Chris observed, drawing level with Stan.

'It's like Brad said,' Stan whined,

turning his head towards Chris. 'No one — '

'I heard.' Chris kept his tone light so as not to alarm his companion. 'Like I said to everyone else — first time for everything.'

'Mister, there's four of them down there,' Stan warned, nodding towards the house.

'I noticed that,' Chris replied. 'That's why we're going to ride in side by side. Hope they like you.'

'Why?'

'Well, if they start shooting,' Chris warned him, not enjoying Stan's discomfort, 'you'll be right in the firing line. And before you think about galloping off — remember. If they don't get you, I will.'

Both men walked their horses down the slight incline, to keep Hardiman between Chris and the waiting waddies.

'What the hell is going on here?' a voice boomed from the interior of the house.

Within seconds the owner of the

voice came out of the house to stand on the porch.

'Sheriff's here to see you, Mr Coleman,' Stan called out, hoping to ease the situation.

'I don't give a damn, Hardiman,' Coleman roared, coming towards the mounted men. 'I gave you and Renton strict instruction. Get your gear and get off my land.'

'Told you,' Stan muttered glumly as he dismounted.

'I don't think that's a good idea, Coleman,' Chris called back, leaning nonchalantly on the pommel of his saddle. 'Stan there did everything he could to stop me. Same goes for the other feller. Well, nearly everything — they could've shot me out of the saddle, but then I don't think you'd like to find yourself linked to another killing.'

Coleman just stared, with disbelief that he had been spoken to like that, at the young sheriff, before signalling him to dismount.

'What happened to Jaeger?' Coleman asked as Chris dismounted and hitched his horse to the rail.

'He got replaced,' Chris told him as he stepped cautiously up on to the veranda.

'I can see that,' Coleman observed, giving Chris a long stare as though weighing him up. 'So where did the town council dig you up from?'

'I volunteered.' Chris offered a warm smile.

'And why would anyone be stupid enough to do that?' Coleman shook his head, as though it was beyond his understanding.

'Mainly, because . . . ' Chris paused, just long enough to make sure that nothing was happening behind him, but the five men in the yard had bunched together. Though alert, they were busy talking amongst themselves. 'Because I want my father's killer behind bars.'

Porter Coleman took a few seconds to absorb this bit of information. Then, slowly, recognition dawned.

'Chris?' he asked, his voice growing husky. 'You came back.'

The pleasure in Coleman's tone baffled Chris as the rancher thrust out his hand. Chris took it in a firm grip. Despite the euphoric outburst, Chris remained calm, his guard up, for he was facing a man who could have been responsible for his father's death.

Coleman seemed relieved as he motioned to the four men and Stan Hardiman who, uncertain about what to do, were still huddled together.

'The man with me is Chris Ford,' Coleman announced. 'Remember him. This man is welcome here.' Then he pointed at two men. 'Bates, Calhoun. You two get down to the gate. Hardiman, I'll deal with you later — and Renton, when he decides to show up.' He glanced over his shoulder at Chris. 'They're a good bunch.'

'Impressed,' Chris cast an admiring look at the waddies. 'You seem to work a tight crew.'

'Wasn't always that way,' Coleman

confessed, staring into the distance. 'We were complete novices, me and your pa, when we came out here. We were apprentices together but I was the one that had the dream. I wanted to be a cattleman — not a cowboy — a rancher, like we read about. Didn't think it'd happen.' He threw a glance at his attentive listener. 'The war came — hell, I didn't think any of us would come through Shiloh. But we did. Your pa and I went all the way through to Appomattox. We thought that if we could do that we could do anything.'

They stood in silence for a while as Coleman, lost in memories of a distant past, stared out over the verdant land. Then, remembering where he was and what he was doing, he turned back to Chris.

'I owed your father too much,' Coleman said, breaking the silence. 'He was like a brother to me. I wouldn't — I couldn't kill him, Chris.'

'Maybe not,' Chris replied thoughtfully. 'But I can't help wondering why you made accusations about him, like you did.'

'That's the trouble, Chris,' Coleman stated with emphasis. 'I know what I'm supposed to have said. That your father was being paid to look the other way as far as the Jaegers were concerned. Except, that never came from me — it's not something I would do.' Coleman began to pace up and down agitatedly while Chris chose to sit on the porch step. 'Things just got out of hand. Sure, I was mad when Tom jailed two of my boys and sent the Jaegers home. But when he explained his actions I could see Tom's point. The same when Tom came to me and said that he didn't want my problems on his streets.'

A pained expression was etched on Coleman's face as he hunkered down beside his friend's son.

'We may have had differences of opinion,' Coleman confessed. 'But we always talked it through. Never got to the point where I'd start rumours or want him dead.'

'Maybe it would be better if you went back to the beginning,' Chris suggested, after digesting everything that he had heard. 'The way I hear it you had help from Aldo Lund but when he buys up the old Stanton place — '

'I know how it looks,' Coleman interrupted, sourly. 'I wanted it all — right from the start. But your father was a fair man. He knew what those carpetbaggers were like. Just didn't think it fair that we left Boyd Stanton and his family with nothing. And, I admit, that I was ignorant and tried to turn a tragedy to my advantage. I didn't know about tick fever. The cattle were there for the taking and, well, I messed up and had to get rid of them. Your father put up the cash for me to buy a new herd and a chap I had dealings with told me to go and talk to Aldo Lund.'

'You went all the way to Mexico?' Chris was a little bemused. 'To ask advice?'

Coleman shook his head: 'No, Lund

had a small place — he called it grazing land. A small place where he could stop off on his way north. He had a thousand head there which he needed to shift. So I bought the herd and he came back with me. Just as well, because he taught me a lot, and he found me a good foreman in Rufus Coverdale. Coverdale was experienced — after all, he was Lund's foreman down there.'

Abruptly, Coleman stood up and stretched himself: 'And, yes, if you really want to know, I was jealous when Aldo bought the Stanton place. I tried to make trouble for them. And, yes, before you ask, I made accusations about them rustling from my herd. But you've got to understand that your father's death brought me to my senses. I realize now that I stood to lose everything if I'd gone to war.'

Chris sighed as he thought through what Coleman had said. 'Yeah,' he said at length, 'he's made a lot of people do a lot of thinking.'

'You should never have gone away,' Coleman blurted out. He swung around to face the lawman, who was rising to his feet. 'He was so damned proud of you. He knew that he should never have pushed you to it.'

'Bit late now,' Chris mumbled. He glanced at the rancher. 'Had to go, anyway. Needed to. If I'd stayed around it would've hung between us. If not by Pa, then by me.'

He hadn't meant to say that but the words had tumbled out. Perhaps, he concluded, it was because they were two men sharing in a common grief. Then again, because Coleman had known his father he had been easier to talk to. No matter what, Chris found himself warming to the rancher. He couldn't define it but there was something about Coleman and Jaeger — their unguarded friendliness and open honesty — that drew Chris to them.

Despite everything, the lawman instinct clicked in. Although he had a picture in his mind that convinced him that neither man had killed his father, nevertheless he had the feeling that they were both involved in some way.

'Chris,' Coleman's voice penetrated his thoughts. 'You've got to find that killer.'

Although Coleman sounded in control, Chris detected a plea.

'You figure you're next?' Chris noticed the pensive look on the rancher's face.

Coleman nodded: 'Don't ask me why — because I have no idea. Just a feeling.'

'Then don't tie my hands,' Chris advised him. 'Think things through — then come and find me. Maybe you and Jaeger can get your story straight. And, before you get het up, I want to hear the bit that, it seems, neither of you wants to tell me.'

'There's nothing to tell,' Coleman said, looking confused. 'I've been straight with you.'

'That you have,' Chris agreed, with a

sardonic look in his eye. 'And, if I read between the lines, I know what the story is. Just prefer it if someone came straight out and said it.'

'If — and it's a big if,' Coleman said with a grin, clapping a hand on Chris's shoulder. 'You think there's something I'm not telling you? OK, if I recall it, I'll come by the office.'

'Fair enough,' Chris said, easily. 'Then I'll be on my way.'

'Maybe I'll drop by tomorrow.' Coleman was more relaxed now. 'Got to see Charlie, anyway. Not looking forward to that chore.'

'Problem?' Chris asked, as he walked towards his horse.

Coleman shook his head: 'Not really. Guess now you're back Hannah gave you all the good news. Figure that Charlie, being the eldest, is my new partner.'

Chris hauled himself up into the saddle and took up the slack in the reins.

'No, he's not,' Chris explained, as he

turned his mount around. 'I am. So I'd be grateful if you didn't send Stan and Renton packing.'

Coleman started laughing: 'You cunning bastard. All along, you knew and you didn't say a word.'

'I got round to it.' Chris pointed out. 'Had more important things to talk about.'

'Fair enough,' Coleman accepted the truth of this. 'I'll give Hardiman and Renton the good news. And I'll make sure that they know that they owe you.'

As Chris rode away, Coleman stood on his porch and watched the retreating figure.

'God, Tom,' he spoke to the sky. 'That boy of yours — just like you when you was his age.'

13

Dusk was falling by the time Chris rode into the livery. He dismounted and stretched before leading the horse into the vacant stall. He was removing the saddle when Uriah Bolton made an appearance.

'Been gone a while,' Uriah commented. He picked up a bag of feed and passed it to Chris.

'Had a lot to talk about,' Chris told him, concentrating on brushing his horse down.

'I take it you got to Coleman, then?' Uriah enquired, his eyebrows rising.

'Yeah,' came the casual reply. 'Tell me, Uriah, how do you reckon things are between Coleman and Jaeger?'

'What's there to say?' the liveryman answered with a nonchalant shrug. 'One minute they was at loggerheads. The next they're like the best of friends.

Mind you, there was a time when they looked set to go to it. Then your pa got hisself killed — and peace broke out. Hell, the pair of them even helped carry the coffin to the graveyard.'

That comment froze Chris. He glanced up with a frown of confusion on his face. He felt as though he was missing something important. He had built up a picture that he thought he could make sense of, but while this new piece of information confirmed it in part, it also created new questions.

'Why would they do that?' he questioned.

'Why not?' Bolton replied, unsure what Chris was hoping for. 'Tom knew them both. When Matt Jaeger turned up Tom was right pleased to see him. Certainly greeted each other like long lost brothers.'

None of this made sense to Chris. He had seen that Coleman and Jaeger were linked through their connection with Aldo Lund. Now there seemed to be a connection between his father and

Jaeger that confounded Chris's logic.

Jaeger was due in town the following day, Chris recalled; he could wait and confront him then. For, now, he had an appointment with an angry young lady. He couldn't afford to have any more problems to cloud his mind.

After saying goodnight to Uriah he walked up the sunset-lit street. As he passed the eating-house he noticed that the blinds had been pulled down. At least, he assumed, Fliss wouldn't see him pass by. But he didn't look up at the second-storey windows.

He entered the office and placed the keys on the hook. Then he stepped back as he noticed that a sawn-down shotgun and a rifle had been added to the rack, weapons that he recognized as belonging to one person. Then, coming from the cells at the back, he caught the sound of someone snoring.

Cautiously, he approached the first cell, then grinned as he held on to the bars and looked at the figure lying on the cot. Hat over his face, belt undone and top button of his pants open, lay Sam Ward.

'Hell's teeth, Chris,' Sam murmured. 'You should know better than to creep up on a sleepin' man.'

'Well, you took a chance yourself,' Chris commented. 'How'd you know I wasn't Matt Jaeger?'

'Because,' Sam replied, taking the hat from his face and swinging round into a sitting position, 'that nice girl over at the eatery told me where to find you. So, you're the new sheriff of this here town?'

'Just trying to find Pa's killer,' Chris explained, as Sam stood up and hitched up his pants.

'Made any headway?' Sam asked, buckling his belt.

'I'm only sure of who didn't kill him,' Chris replied, walking back to the office.

'Not Coleman or Jaeger?' Sam asked. He followed Chris to the office and slumped down in the chair in front of the desk.

'They're involved,' Chris explained, wiping his tired face with his hand. 'But I don't think they are involved in the killing.' Then another thought struck him. 'Remember Rufus Coverdale?'

'Coverdale? Haven't heard that name in years,' Sam made a whooshing noise as he recalled the name. 'Smalltime rancher, as I recall. Sold out to a feller called Scott Murphy. Why?'

Chris shook his head: 'Coverdale didn't own the ranch. Aldo Lund did. Used it as a staging post to fatten up his cattle before driving them north.'

Sam absorbed this fact, then grinned: 'And hide a few head of stolen cattle? Hell of an idea that — hidin' the herd right in plain sight.'

Chris nodded: 'That's what I figure. When Coleman met up with him, Lund said that he had a thousand head that he needed to shift.'

'So you figure that Coleman built his empire on stolen cattle?' Sam leaned forward so that he could see Chris's face.

'And he probably knew they were stolen,' Chris added. 'You know what gets me? My pa, for all his faults, was always a straight and honest man. I can't believe he'd be a party to a deal like that.'

'Maybe, Chris, that's the problem,' Sam observed thoughtfully. 'Maybe he didn't know. With Jaeger around and knowing the truth it'd make sense if Coleman killed *him*. He'd want to shut Jaeger up so'd he couldn't make trouble for him. I just don't see a motive for killing your pa.'

Chris gave Sam a long, suspicious look. 'You seem a bit well-informed, Sam. You know something that I don't? If you do, then please, don't hold out on me.'

'Chris, this is serious business,' Sam explained. 'Tom Carrick and me had a talk about things — he filled in some of the gaps, but that's all. I got nothin' new to tell you — nothin' that you ain't figured out already.'

'Except for one thing,' Chris pointed

out. 'Coleman thinks that whoever killed my pa will come for him, too.'

Sam's eyes narrowed as he took that piece of information in: 'Any evidence for that?'

'Only a gut instinct that says that the killer's in town,' Chris answered. 'But I know most of the people and can't see any of them bearing a grudge.'

'Maybe I'll do some listening,' Sam offered. 'After all, you ain't been around for five years. Never know what might have happened in that time.'

'Fair enough,' Chris conceded. Then a thought struck him. 'You got a place to sleep tonight?'

'I'll bunk down here,' Sam replied. 'Now you get along home and washed up. I hear you have a liaison with a young lady tonight.'

'Yeah, right,' Chris scowled. 'But liaison it won't be.'

'Just treat her right, Chris,' Sam advised, with a faint grin. 'Way I hear it she packs a strong right hand.'

Chris stopped dead in his tracks,

spun around and stabbed a finger at Sam: 'You know, you can go off people. You make any more comments like that..'

He stopped and threw his hands in the air as though dismissing the subject. Sam's sudden burst of laughter did nothing to soothe his irritation and still rang in Chris's ears as he walked home. Then he too began to chuckle as the funny side of things registered. It was good that Sam was here in Stanton for Chris was certain that together they would bring his father's killer to book.

★　★　★

Later, washed and dressed in his preferred blue shirt and denims, Chris entered the eating-house. Standing there, with the door closed behind him, he looked at the scattering of round tables with their pale-blue gingham covers. In the centre was a table set for two with an unlit candle as a centrepiece.

Out back, beyond the counter and behind a gingham curtain, he could hear a dog bark. The sound was curtailed by a soft shooshing sound. So, Wolfie was still around, he mused, as his mind went back six years to when Felicity had fallen love with the Alsatian pup he had bought for her. He crossed the room, flicked aside the curtain and entered the kitchen. Immediately, the dog lunged forward, leaping high and pinning him to the wall with its paws on his shoulders, while a long, wet tongue flicked across his face.

'Hallo, fella. You still remember me?' he greeted the dog as he ruffled the fur around its ears.

'Just goes to show,' Felicity commented evenly. 'Once seen never forgotten.'

Chris could detect a faint barb in her comment and found himself unable to deal with it. He was not used to dealing with the opposite sex. The only girl that he had truly known was the one he was with now.

'Smells good.' He tried to divert the conversation, as the contented dog sat at his feet.

'Nothing special.' Felicity was thawing — just a little. 'Beef pie..' she faltered as she gave him a peculiar look. 'Don't try to sweet-talk me, Christopher Ford, I'm not in the mood.'

'Obviously, it's something I've done.' Chris tried to keep his tone light, but it didn't impress her much.

'Typical male,' Fliss huffed. 'Do you really need it spelling out?'

'Let me guess,' Chris snapped back, rubbing thoughtfully at his chin. 'You figure I ran out on you? Hell, Fliss, we were just friends — weren't we? Besides, look at what I did — I figured after that you'd have no time for me.'

Fliss looked at him as she heard the boy in him, the boy whom she had known who now stood there in a man's body.

'What you did was wrong,' Felicity said, softly, as she approached him. 'Even if it was for the right reasons.

Only you know the answer to that — but I wouldn't have condemned you for it. Chris, there was a time when we could talk to each other. When you went away, I was hurt, but I lived for the day you'd see sense and come back. And when you didn't I tried to get on with my life. Running this place helps. But not at night . . . ' Her voice faded to a whisper. 'I was so happy when Joe told me you were back. I know it's because your pa got killed.' Then she slammed a fist into his chest as anger lit her next words. 'But you didn't give me a thought, did you? What were you thinking? Ride in and ride out again without giving me another thought?'

'Hell, Fliss, I don't know,' Chris yelled, grabbing her wrists. 'But some things cut both ways. I didn't know if you wanted to see me. All you had to do was come over to the office — or the house — if you were that bothered.' Realizing that he could be hurting her, he let Fliss go. 'Look, Fliss, I've got enough on my plate without being

241

bothered about — '

'Someone who loves you?' Fliss threw in.

This remark reduced Chris to silence. This was something that he felt unable to deal with.

'Fliss,' he murmured at last. 'Fliss, I don't know what to do. Or what to say.'

'Because it's not manly to have emotions?' Fliss challenged, staring into his wavering eyes.

'Not that.' He stared at the panting dog with its lolling tongue. 'But I can't handle this right now.' He took a deep breath. 'When — when all this is over I'll make time for us. Talk things through. And, I promise you, I won't run away.'

'I'll hold you to that,' Fliss whispered. She reached out and squeezed his hand.

'I'd better go, then.' Chris backed away towards the curtain.

'You could.' Fliss turned back to the oven. 'But you'd waste a good meal and not find out, tonight, about the night your pa got killed.'

This remark left Chris stunned. Conflicting emotions flickered across his face. He was unsure what he should do next. He was angry that Fliss had said nothing sooner, yet he understood that she might have been worried about how he would take it, he was also relieved that there might be someone who could shed more light on the matter.

'See, Chris, we have the same problem,' Fliss continued, not enjoying the moment as she set out the warmed plates that she had removed from the stove. 'We're both stubborn. Bet you ignored Uriah and K when they asked if you'd seen me. I had to do something to grab your attention.'

'Ain't going to argue with you,' Chris surrendered. 'Maybe I deserve the slap and that you're angry with me. But not telling me about Pa . . . ' He left the rest unsaid as he waved towards the curtained doorway. 'I'm here now. I'll wait out there until you're ready.'

He sat at the table in a state of confusion. He felt as though he had wasted the day trying to piece things together, in looking for a motive and a suspect for his father's death. Although a picture was forming that exonerated the two main protagonists, he could not help but think that he should have put his pride to one side. Had he not been so concerned about avoiding Felicity, he might have had additional information with which to work.

'Let's start again,' he said decisively when Fliss emerged with two plates piled high with beef pie, potatoes and fresh cabbage.

'You mean you want me to slap you again?' she asked, lightly. She placed his plate in front of him.

'Er — no,' he said, leaning back in case she mistook his meaning. 'I meant — '

'I know what you meant,' she teased, as she sat down. 'So, how have you been?'

He would rather have talked about

the events surrounding his father's death. Instead, he found himself drawn towards Fliss, as he recounted his life since they had last met. In return, she gave him a brief account of how things had been with her. Slowly, he thawed and the meal was eaten by two people who had known each other most of their lives.

When she brought him a slice of apple pie he found it difficult to refuse. When she said that it was cooked according to his mother's recipe he had to smile as he recalled Fliss learning how to cook in his mother's kitchen.

After she had cleared the table and brought in two cups of coffee the conversation became more serious. And he was ready to listen calmly to what she had to say.

'Every evening I take Wolfie out,' she began. 'We go up to the cemetery and back. As I was coming back I saw your father outside the saloon. There were three or four men riding out of town. I saw Rufus Coverdale come out of the saloon and have a few words with your father. Across the road I saw Porter Coleman, carrying a saddle, walk towards the two men . . . ' She held her hand up to stop him asking a question. 'Let me finish. As I got closer I heard Coleman tell Coverdale to follow him down to the livery. They had not got far when a shot was fired. I think it came from the alley by the sheriff's office. Coleman dropped his saddle, drew his gun and ran towards the office. Coverdale rode across the street, straight up the alley. They didn't find anybody. Then a crowd began to appear at the windows. Coleman picked up his saddle and ran down the street, followed by Coverdale. I took Wolfie home and then ran down to the livery. Coverdale had Uriah pinned up against the wall and Coleman was talking to him. Told him to say nothing. Coleman was worried that if people found out he was in town they'd pin your father's death on him. So, you see, it was important to Uriah that you should talk to me. Whatever happened, it wasn't Coleman or Coverdale who killed your father.'

Chris sat in silence as he thought through what she had told him. He could understand Coleman's actions but it would have been much better if he had confessed to being in town. All Fliss had done was confirm his own gut feeling that the killer was right here in town.

'I think I saw the killer,' she said hesitantly, uncertain how he would react. 'But I don't know who he is.'

'What did he look like?' Chris asked, hoping a description would give him an idea of where to look.

'You remember when we were kids?' Fliss asked. 'There used to be that strange kid with the hair that covered his face. You know, it just flopped down? He had a spotty chin — always picking at it? Tall and thin. That's what he looked like — the man at the back of the stores. His hair had flopped down but his lower face — he had something wrapped around it.'

Chris shook his head: 'I know who you mean. But I can't place him. He was older than us? Yes?'

'I think so.' Fliss tried hard to recall the boy. 'I don't think he was at school. Sometimes when we came out he'd be standing there. Gave me the creeps. So did that man that night. I mean, as I got closer, he . . . well, he just disappeared. I ran out into the street and he'd just vanished.'

'And you've not mentioned this to anyone?' Chris asked with concern.

'I did say something to Uriah,' Fliss confessed. 'He said that the boy could've been Roy Stanton. You know, the boy who found me?' and, when Chris nodded as he recalled the incident, continued. 'Uriah said it couldn't be him. He said that if that boy had come back Uriah would've known about it.'

'Well, if he has,' Chris laid his hands on hers; an unconscious act that she made no attempt to stop. 'Then someone has to know where he is. I wouldn't let it worry you. Somehow, and don't ask me why, but I don't think you'll come to any harm.'

As they talked about their childhood, so it drew in other memories. When it became quite late they extinguished the lamps before abandoning the restaurant for the comfort of the small parlour upstairs. There they continued to catch up with each other.

Eventually, they turned out the lights.

At the back of the eating-house, hidden in the shadows, a man began to weep. Slowly, bitterly he walked away.

'Make the most of this night,' he whispered into the night. 'Tomorrow you will be dead. Felicity belongs to me.'

14

It was a happy and contented man who walked out of Fliss's eating house, his belly full with a generous portion of bacon and eggs. Maybe he could be excused for looking on the world with a rosy glow, for he had built several bridges. He and Fliss had reminisced and taken their interrupted relationship a few steps further.

He had a job, a girl and a home. It was, he thought, good to be alive.

'I take it you've seen Fliss?' Katy's voice took him by surprise.

He just smiled and nodded before crossing the street towards the sheriff's office. It was best to leave Katy to make her own assumptions.

Sam was already up when he walked into the office. There was coffee bubbling on the stove and Sam was sitting at the desk with a cup in front of him.

'So — who didn't go home last night?' Sam asked, with a twinkle in his eye. 'You've made a catch there. Does a decent apple pie.'

'She would do,' Chris acknowledged, pouring himself a cup of coffee. 'Ma showed her how to do it.'

'Don't know how you could've left a girl like that,' Sam observed, choosing his words carefully. 'And before you ask, I had a couple of beers over at the saloon. That K, she's a mighty fine woman.'

'Bit young for you,' Chris quipped, not being drawn in the direction Sam wanted him to go.

'Only by a few years,' Sam pointed out. He felt a tad hurt that Chris should bring age into it.

'That's true,' Chris agreed.

'You know, I was thinking,' Sam said, looking out of the window. 'This is what I need. A small town sheriff's job. It'd see me through.'

'Unfortunately, this town has a sheriff,' Chris stated. 'But I know what you mean.'

'Sounds kind of permanent,' Sam frowned.

'I could always take on a deputy, you know,' Chris said, his face deadpan, but unable to keep a touch of humour out of his tone.

'Hell's teeth.' Sam chuckled, shaking his head. 'I think you're damned serious.'

'I guess I am, at that,' Chris said, seriously. 'It's not much, but it'd give you time to sort out what you want to do. The law's the only thing you know — '

Sam held up his hand to silence his partner.

'I appreciate what you're sayin', Chris. Really do,' Sam sounded truely grateful. 'But you'd best forget all that stuff I said awhiles back. There's still life in this old horse yet.'

'Yeah, guess there is,' Chris conceded, without making the comment sound like an apology.

Outside, the Carfax stage rattled its way down the street to halt outside the livery. Chris strolled outside and leaned against the doorjamb to watch the passengers disembark. There were two drummers with their cases, a husband and wife, and another man in a suit who could be anything. All five trooped up the street and entered the eating-house.

Down at the livery the driver and Uriah Bolton worked at releasing the horses from the harness, while the rather youthful-looking guard just stood by and watched. Only when the chore was completed did driver and guard amble up towards the saloon. It was evident that there was no teamwork between them, for the driver looked to be berating the younger man.

From the corner of his eye Chris caught sight of some movement. Two riders were coming down the trail. Chris pushed himself away from the doorjamb and turned to go back into the office. Charlie chose this moment to climb up on to the boardwalk.

'I need to talk to you,' Charlie

blurted out, anxious to have his brother's attention.

'It's not a good time,' Chris told him coldly. He glanced over his shoulder to see the two riders drawing towards the livery.

'Sam,' Chris called. 'Time to go for a walk.'

'A walk?' Sam queried, rising up.

'Fogarty has come to town,' Chris cast him a crafty look. 'Thought you'd want to meet him.'

'Not my jurisdiction,' Sam nodded, moving to the gun rack and taking down his sawn-off shotgun.

'He's in mine,' Chris quipped.

'Of course he is,' Sam acknowledged with a wry grin. He approached the door and peered around it. 'And Matt Jaeger, I see.'

'We did a deal,' Chris informed him. 'Jaeger's brought Fogarty in. Couldn't ask him to do more than that. He has an amnesty in return.'

'Your decision,' Sam conceded. 'Not wearing your coat?'

'Best to shuck that duster,' Chris explained. 'Don't want to be recognized straight off. I want to do this peaceful without anyone doing any shooting.'

'Not much chance of that,' Charlie observed from the door. 'Looks like they've got back-up.'

Chris peered around the door to see three more men riding, fast, towards town.

'The one in the black coat,' Charlie was quick to inform his brother, 'that's Billy McDonald.'

'Damn, he's posted out of town,' Chris barked, angrily.

'Come on, Chris.' Sam stepped through the door. 'Let's get down there and see if we can't sort this out.'

'I'm coming with you,' Charlie announced. He ran into the office and grabbed his father's Henry rifle from the rack.

But the first two men had gone ahead and were halfway towards the livery before Charlie caught up with them. Chris knew that he should have sent

Charlie packing but it was too late. Now the three of them were facing five men.

Matt Jaeger was unaware that the lawmen were behind him. He was too busy telling the others to go back to the ranch.

'No one tells me where I can and can't go,' Billy McDonald was yelling at his boss.

'Billy's right, Pa.' Clint backed up his friend. 'We're not the ones who should be posted out of town.'

'Just get, all of you,' Matt demanded of them.

Behind him, Fogarty was staring at Sam Ward. It took a few seconds for him to register that the marshal was alive and well and standing right in front of him.

'I was told you was dead,' Fogarty yelled, snatching at his holstered pistol.

Matt Jaeger began to turn around. At that moment Charlie pulled the trigger of the Henry. Coldly and deliberately he shot Billy McDonald. Stunned, everybody froze for long enough to see McDonald spin around and crash to the ground. Fogarty was the first to recover. He drew his gun. At the same moment Sam brought up his shotgun. It belched two barrels of shot that shredded Fogarty just as his own gun cleared the holster. Part of the spread ripped into Jaeger's right arm, which he grabbed as he swung back.

'Don't fire,' he yelled at Buell and Clint Jaeger, both of whom were in the process of drawing their guns.

Chris, shocked by what was happening, turned on his brother in an attempt to grab the rifle from him. But Charlie backed away, his face dark and looking as though he was prepared to use the rifle on Chris should that prove necessary.

'What the hell are you doing?' Chris screamed at him.

'Billy McDonald,' Charlie yelled back, trying to fight Chris off. 'He's the one that killed Pa.'

Then Chris felt a burning pain across

his back. Twisting round, he scrabbled for his own pistol. As he did this he saw that it was Buell who was firing at him, but the bullets were going wide. Chris, despite feeling a rising panic, managed to keep calm himself long enough to get off two shots. He saw Buell go down, his last bullet going into the ground. Or it seemed to, but Matt Jaeger suddenly went down on to one knee as though his left leg had been shot out from under him. Despite his wounds, Jaeger managed to keep his hands in the air.

Behind Chris the rifle roared again and Clint, who had done as his father had asked and holstered his gun, doubled over. Toppling to the ground, he lay there squirming and screaming, his feet drumming against the packed earth as his father crawled towards him.

'This didn't have to happen,' Chris roared. He threw his gun away and advanced on Charlie.

'That bastard killed our pa,' Charlie screamed back. 'Everybody saw him with a gun in his hand. They saw him kill Pa.'

All the rage, all the feelings that he hoped that he would never experience again were in the punch that lifted Charlie from his feet and sent him sprawling. Unlike his father, Charlie did not get back on his feet. Instead, he scrabbled away until he came up against something solid. Looking up, he saw Hal standing there.

'Did you see what he done, Hal?' Charlie whined, grabbing his youngest brother's leg.

'I saw,' Hal glared down at him and pulled his leg away. 'And it was a long time coming.'

Dropping his head, Charlie crawled towards the stage and used a wheel to pull himself up.

'You all right, Chris?' Hal asked, with concern.

'Yeah, I need a board or something.' Chris waved behind him. 'Got to get the wounded to the doctor.'

'See what I can find,' Hal promised,

running back to the site.

Chris turned back to face the carnage. Uriah had come out of the livery and was attending to Clint by applying a padded bandage to the wound in his stomach. Sam had ripped open Matt Jaeger's pants and was using a sleeve from Matt's shirt to bind the leg wound.

Fliss was there, too, down on her knees helping Uriah, who was joined by a young man with a medical bag.

At least, Chris thought, someone had had the sense to call the doctor.

Everything seemed to be taking on a dreamlike quality. Hal came over with a door, which he laid on the ground. Then he helped Uriah and the doctor to put Clint on it. Matt Jaeger, supported by Sam, came passing by. They paused for a moment to allow Matt to pass Chris his gun. He said something but Chris couldn't hear what he was saying; the mouth shapes seemed to say that no one could blame him for what had happened.

Uriah and a couple of men from the building site carried the door, with Clint Jaeger on it, up the street. Hal and Fliss detached themselves from the crowd, before coming to his side.

'Got to find Charlie,' Chris murmured. 'Got to find him before he does something stupid.'

'No, you don't,' Hal told him firmly. 'You can't keep on running after him.'

'Taking the blame for him,' Fliss added.

'That's what got you messed up before,' Hal reminded him, with a look of concern.

Chris nodded, as though he understood: 'Figure you're right. He started this mess — and he'll have to pay for it.'

'Then do the job you asked for.' Fliss made the suggestion sound like an order. 'Sam's on his own, holding the fort for you.'

Chris walked up the street looking neither left or right at the bystanders who had seen the peace of their town shattered. The same people who had given him condemning looks when he had struck out at his father.

He came to a halt, lifted his head and looked around him. As he did so, so the accusing looks faded away as the townsfolk looked anywhere but at him.

'Once in a while,' he said to the crowd, 'killing is a necessary evil. But what you saw today — that was coldblooded murder. As citizens of this town, if you see Charlie Ford you will report his whereabouts to me.'

'And you'll do what?' a voice from the crowd called out.

'He'll stand trial for murder,' Chris stated, the firmness in his tone making everyone know that he meant every word. 'When a man does wrong, in my book, he doesn't walk away unpunished. I don't care about his standing in the community. Remember that.'

Silence was the response as Chris turned away and strode towards his office. There he found his way barred by Fred Harris and two of the council men.

'I know you asked for the badge until you caught your pa's killer,' Harris said, boldly. 'But we'd be grateful if you'd consider staying on as the law here.'

Chris produced a wry smile: 'I'll give it my consideration.'

★　★　★

The inside of the office looked more like a field hospital. The doctor, with blood up to his elbows, was operating on Clint's body, which occupied the top of the sheriff's desk. Matt was seated on a cot in the cell, with Uriah using the doctor's tweezers to pull out pieces of shot that were embedded in his right arm. Jaeger's pants had gone so that his leg wound could be cauterized and dressed.

'Doc don't figure Clint'll make it,' Matt confessed, sadly. 'Bullet just ripped up his guts.'

'I'm just sorry it came to this,' Chris said. His tone sounded apologetic.

'Ain't your doin',' Matt said with a

263

shake of his head. 'It was that damned brother of yours. And that fool Fogarty — should've listened to my boys and sent him packin'.' He looked up at Sam, who was leaning against the bars. 'I suppose you'll be wantin' to take me in, Sam?'

'That's up to the law,' Sam said, grimly. 'But I ain't the law here — so I've got no say.'

'Thanks, Sam.' Matt sighed, then jerked as another piece of shot was wrenched from his flesh. 'I suppose someone should get word to Perry. Tell him what happened.'

'I wouldn't,' Uriah snapped. 'We don't need another bloodbath.'

Matt could see the sense in that. Telling Perry was something that he would have to deal with later.

'What the hell has been going on?' a new voice called out, forcing everybody to look at the speaker.

Standing in the doorway was Porter Coleman, with his foreman standing behind him.

'You could say a number of chickens coming home to roost,' Sam Ward suggested.

'Hope this isn't going to be laid at my door.' Coleman's tone was stern but wary.

'Should it?' Chris asked.

'I only came to town,' Coleman decided that it was better that he came to the point, 'to tell you something that I recalled. That rumour about your pa taking a backhander. Like I said, it never came from me. Never heard it before — not until someone asked me if I thought that Tom could be being bribed. I didn't give that idea the time of day — I think I may have made a dismissive noise.'

'Sounds like Charlie,' Chris suggested. 'Grunt and he'd take it as a 'yes'.'

'Not Charlie,' Coleman dismissed that idea. 'I'd give him an emphatic 'no'.'

Outside the office there was a sudden commotion as a woman screamed and other voices shouted out a warning. The window shattered as two shots came through; one of which caught Coleman while the other missed Chris by a fraction of an inch and embedded itself in the wall.

Chris, Sam and Rufus Coverdale acted as one as they recovered from the shock, drew their weapons and hurtled themselves out into the street. There many fingers were pointing up the alley that ran alongside the sheriff's office.

Leaving Coverdale to cover the front of the office, Sam and Chris went towards the back. Sam held up his hand and pointed to the ground, where fresh footprints showed that the killer had run up and around the backs of the buildings. They did not have to follow them far, for they found that the tracks led to the building three doors up from the office.

Chris signalled to Sam to remain where he was. Then, using his fingers, he indicated that he was going round the front.

A few seconds later Chris entered the leather-goods store. Ryan Eckersley stood behind the counter; his greased hair had fallen down over his face. Nervously, the middle finger of his hand reached up to scrape at his beard — like a boy picking at the scabs on his spots.

'I knew you'd come back,' he breathed, heavily. 'You took Fliss away from me. I found her — remember? She was mine.'

'You killed my father,' Chris said with incredulity, 'to get me to come back so that you could kill me?'

'Why not?' Eckersley spoke with an airy confidence that suggested that he thought he was in command. 'You are just the icing on the cake. But I would have preferred it if you had killed Coleman first.'

'Why?' Chris showed that he was confused. 'Why would I want to do that?'

'All the evidence was there,' Eckersley explained, as though to a schoolboy.

'The rumours and, I'm sure Fliss told you, Coleman was out there the night your father died. He had been here to collect a saddle.'

'Still don't see a reason for me to kill Coleman,' Chris pointed out.

'Coleman killed my father,' Eckersley blurted out. 'Oh, and don't insult my intelligence by telling me that he committed suicide. It wouldn't have happened if that Porter Coleman had not destroyed everything that my father had.'

'And, before you ask, and to be honest, I had hoped that those no account Jaegers would have done the job. There was bad blood there and I really believed that killing your father would tip both them and Coleman into a full-blown war. I just don't understand why that didn't happen.'

Chris did not respond, for he had listened to Eckersley's explanation with interest. He knew, also, that Fliss had been right but the changes in the man who stood in front of him were such that, had he passed him in the street, he would not have recognized him. Just as nothing had been triggered when Chris had met Eckersley at the meeting of the Town Council.

Now Chris knew from Eckersley's account that the owner of the leather-goods store was Boyd Stanton's son, Roy.

'It didn't have to be this way,' Chris stated, sadly. 'All you've done is create a load of havoc and got people killed. I've got no choice but to arrest you for the murder of my father.'

'I do not think so,' Stanton responded, harshly, producing his gun from below the counter and pointing it at Chris. 'Our business isn't finished. You still stand between Fliss and me.'

'Then you'll not be seeing her again,' Sam, who had crept in the back way and listened in, informed Roy Stanton.

Stanton's head dropped, his face pale as he stepped back, leaving his gun on the counter.

'So you win again,' Stanton said sullenly.

Chris shook his head: 'No, Roy, just doing my job.'

Together, Chris and Sam escorted a handcuffed Roy Stanton down to the sheriff's office. Anxious and inquisitive townsfolk gathered around the prisoner and escort. People who began to express their anger as the rumour began to spread that the lawman had caught Tom Ford's killer.

'Hell's teeth,' Sam muttered, once they closed the door. 'We're goin' to have to get this feller out of town tonight. Else there's goin' to be a lynch mob hammerin' on the door.'

'We'll need someone here, if we do,' Chris pointed out, as he pushed Stanton into the far cell and locked the door.

'If it's of any help,' the doctor put in, 'I've one patient I can't move.'

'And I'm not leavin' my boy,' Matt added.

'All I have is a sprained wrist,'

Coleman blurted out. 'And a hole in the fleshy part of my arm. So Rufus and I can stay in town tonight — if you want us.'

'Well, Porter, Matt, that sounds right neighbourly of you both,' Chris had a mischievous look about him as he approached the two men. 'I mean, one minute you were arranging a range war and the next the pair of you were carrying my pa's coffin like you were the best of friends. I've got to ask the question — why?'

'Respect,' Coleman supplied.

'Obviously,' Chris continued to grin. 'I mean a man falls on hard times and goes to see Matt, here, and tells his sorry little tale. Matt says that he can help this feller out, after all, he's got a thousand stolen steers he has to shift. What was it, Porter, a cheap deal? Or just that you didn't want Pa knowing that he was making a profit out of stolen beef.'

'I'm just glad your father isn't around to hear what you just said,' Coleman responded, petulantly. 'He'd be mad as hell to know that was what happened. And, before you draw any more conclusions, I would've preferred it if Matt had not moved on to the old Stanton place.'

'So you knew where to find Matt, then?' Chris asked, knowing that he was getting closer to the truth.

'Leave it, Chris,' Matt suggested. 'You've worked out the story.'

'Then why not finish it?' asked Sam, who had been listening to the exchange with interest. 'Don't you think Chris is old enough to hear a story about three Union soldiers?'

Coleman and Matt Jaeger exchanged glances before Matt said: 'Sounds like this feller's been talking to the Major.'

Sam nodded as he confirmed: 'Me and Al Jennings spent some time together.' Then he turned to Chris and explained: 'He's the doctor in Carfax. Knew the three of them quite well.'

'Well, now that we've got everything settled,' Chris suggested. 'I think we'd best shift Stanton while there's still daylight. At least it'll discourage any lynch mob.'

'That's a very good point,' Uriah agreed, anxious to be a part of what was going on. 'I'll go fetch up some horses.'

As he left, Fliss took Chris by one arm and drew him outside.

'Is it all over?' she asked pensively.

'Yes,' Chris assured her. 'And you were right. Ryan Eckersley was Roy Stanton.'

'The boy who found me?' she questioned. 'But why would he want to kill your father?'

'Revenge,' Chris advised. Whatever else he meant to say was forgotten as he lifted his eyes to watch a rider approach.

Perry Jaeger came riding up the street, leading another horse with a blanket-covered corpse across the saddle.

'Just what the hell's goin' on here,' Perry demanded as he drew level, then jerked his thumb over his shoulder. 'That there's your brother. Had no choice but to shoot Charlie down. Just came chargin' up to the house hollerin' about how we killed your pa and blastin' away at anythin' that moved. Killed my grandpa and one of the hands has a bullet in his shoulder.'

As he finished speaking, Perry dismounted and then stepped to one side.

'Now, if you got a grudge against my kin,' Perry continued as he dropped into a crouch with his hand hovering over the butt of his gun, 'then best we finish it here and now.'

Before Chris could offer an explanation Perry was distracted as Matt Jaeger hobbled out of the sheriff's office and stood on the boardwalk glowering down at his son.

'There's been enough killing, Perry,' he roared then added, in a weary tone. 'Let's have no more stupidity. Clint's in there and the doc reckons he won't last the night.'

Perry glowered at Chris before following his father into the office.

As they went in, so Sam and Uriah came out. Without saying a word Uriah went to the horse bearing the corpse and led it up towards the undertaker's shop.

'Got some things to do first,' Chris advised Sam. 'Charlie's got himself killed. Just didn't listen and went off half-cocked. I guess I'll have to break the news to Ma.'

'Well, I need to get back,' Sam reminded him. 'That's if I got a job to go back to. Well, at least, we caught up with Fogarty.'

'We did,' Chris acknowledged.

Sam stared down the street sensing an awkwardness between them.

'Figure you won't be coming back,' Sam mentioned, wistfully. 'Should've realized that all along.'

Chris shook his head: 'I'm the sheriff here, now. Besides, this is my home.'

'I thought — ' Sam began, faltering as he tried to find the words.

'I quit, Sam, remember?' Chris gently reminded him.

'Hell's teeth, Chris,' Sam blurted out. 'I didn't think you meant it else I would've asked for the badge back.'

'Well, I didn't think of that either,' Chris admitted. 'Only had one thing on my mind at the time.'

Sam smiled, sadly, as he clapped Chris on the shoulder: 'Anyway we get to ride together one more time.'

'We do,' Chris acknowledged. 'But I'd best go talk to Ma, first.'

Dreading that moment he turned away and began to walk up the street. He had hardly taken a few steps when Fliss caught up with him and looped her arm through his. This was something that they were going to do together.

We do hope that you have enjoyed reading this large print book.

Did you know that all of our titles are available for purchase?

We publish a wide range of high quality large print books including:
Romances, Mysteries, Classics
General Fiction
Non Fiction and Westerns

Special interest titles available in large print are:
The Little Oxford Dictionary
Music Book, Song Book
Hymn Book, Service Book

Also available from us courtesy of Oxford University Press:
Young Readers' Dictionary
(large print edition)
Young Readers' Thesaurus
(large print edition)

For further information or a free brochure, please contact us at:
Ulverscroft Large Print Books Ltd.,
The Green, Bradgate Road, Anstey,
Leicester, LE7 7FU, England.
Tel: (00 44) **0116 236 4325**
Fax: (00 44) **0116 234 0205**

Other titles in the
Linford Western Library:

LIGHTNING AT THE HANGING TREE

Mark Falcon

Mike Clancey was the name inside the rider's watch, but many people during his travels called him Lightning. He was too late to stop a hanging, the men were far away when he reached the lonely swinging figure of a middle-aged man. Then a youth rode up and Lightning found out that the hanged man was his father. So why had he been hanged? Soon the two were to ride together in a pitiless search for the killers.

YUMA BREAKOUT

Jeff Sadler

Horseless and down to his last dollar, out-of-work cowpuncher Nahum Crabtree ended up in the small town of Rios. After a spell in jail, he thought his fortunes had improved when a freighting outfit took him on, especially when one of his bosses turned out to be an attractive young woman. Yes, everything was going well — until he became unwittingly involved in springing a convict from Yuma Penitentiary. And that was only the beginning of his troubles . . .

ROGUE LAW

Logan Winters

The corrupt town of Montero wanted Julius Lang as marshal, but he refused the work as too dangerous and no job for an upright man. When persuasion didn't work, the town took Lang's ranch from him. And when pretty Matti Ullman arrived to lay claim to his land, Lang, needing to earn a living, was forced into the marshal's job. So Montero got Lang as their marshal — and they expected compliance — but what they got was rogue law . . .

A GUNFIGHT TOO MANY

Chap O'Keefe

Sheriff Sam Hammond, nearing his half-century, sometimes wonders just why he became a lawman. Then the troubles really begin: firstly he narrowly escapes death after a gun battle with rustlers; then the gun-handy range detective Herb Hopkirk shoots dead a rash cowpoke, cripples Sam's deputy, Clint Freeman, and pesters rancher John Snyder's daughter, Sarah. When a mysterious bank robber and a man-hungry widow add to his headaches, is it time for him to quit before he winds up dead?

IN THE NAME OF THE GUN

Ryan Bodie

Nobody saw him appear, but suddenly he was there on the street, the rising sun at his back casting his shadow across the dust. 'Shiloh!' Either one man called his name or a dozen whispered it at once. That single word saw Cleveland Kain step from the alley, .45 glinting in the early light. 'Shiloh can't beat Kain,' gasped the judge. 'Nobody can.' 'Can and will!' Shakespeare Jones said loudly. Then whispered: 'If he doesn't this town is doomed!'